SEABORNE

STRANGERS
IN ATLANTIS

SEABORNE

BOOK TWO

STRANGERS IN ATLANTIS

MATT MYKLUSCH

🍂 CAROLRHODA BOOKS

MINNEAPOLIS

Carolrhoda Books
A division of Lerner Publishing Group, Inc.
241 First Avenue North
Minneapolis, MN 55401 USA

For reading levels and more information, look up this title at www.lernerbooks.com.

Jacket illustration by Matthew Armstrong.
Cover and interior images: © Volodymyr Leus/Shutterstock.com (banner); © Laura Westlund/Independent Picture Service (blueprint).

Main body text set in Adobe Caslon Pro Regular 12/19.
Typeface provided by Adobe Systems.

Library of Congress Cataloging-in-Publication Data

Names: Myklusch, Matt, author.
Title: Strangers in Atlantis / Matt Myklusch.
Description: Minneapolis : Carolrhoda Books, [2017] | Series: Seaborne ; book 2 | Summary: "Reformed pirate Dean Seaborne is blackmailed into one last job. Dean must rob a secret resort for globetrotting royals. When he tries, he discovers an underwater kingdom below: Atlantis, on the brink of civil war" —Provided by publisher.
Identifiers: LCCN 2016021192 (print) | LCCN 2016037723 (ebook) | ISBN 9781512413755 (th : alk. paper) | ISBN 9781512426915 (eb pdf)
Subjects: LCSH: Atlantis (Legendary place)—Juvenile fiction. | CYAC: Atlantis (Legendary place)—Fiction. | Pirates—Fiction. | Spies—Fiction.
Classification: LCC PZ7.M994 St 2017 (print) | LCC PZ7.M994 (ebook) | DDC [Fic]—dc23

LC record available at https://lccn.loc.gov/2016021192

Manufactured in the United States of America
1-39814-21336-10/3/2016

For my mom, whose heart is bigger than the ocean

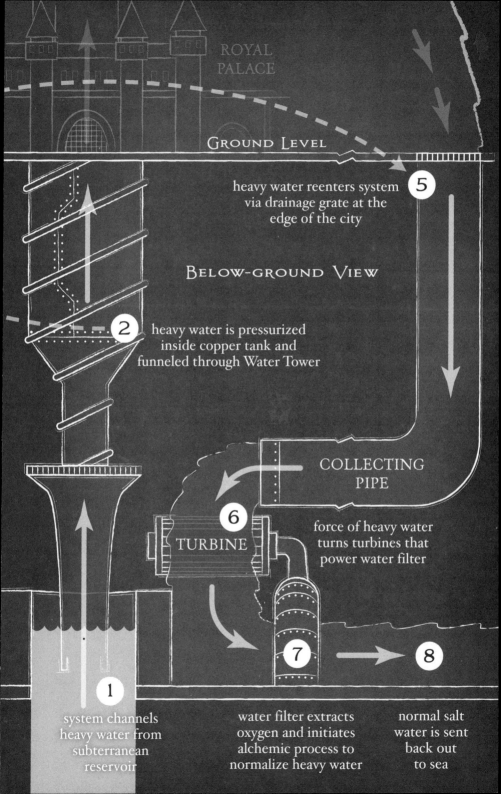

ROYAL PALACE

GROUND LEVEL

5 heavy water reenters system via drainage grate at the edge of the city

BELOW-GROUND VIEW

2 heavy water is pressurized inside copper tank and funneled through Water Tower

COLLECTING PIPE

6 TURBINE

force of heavy water turns turbines that power water filter

1 system channels heavy water from subterranean reservoir

7 **8**

water filter extracts oxygen and initiates alchemic process to normalize heavy water

normal salt water is sent back out to sea

PART ONE

NOWHERE TO RUN

CHAPTER 1

TROUBLE IN PARADISE

"I'm telling you, Seaborne, that girl wants you dead."

Dean Seaborne's eyebrows went up. "What?"

Ronan shrugged as if he'd said the most obvious thing in the world. "If not, I'm confused. Looks to me she's doing her best to get you killed. That's not even the worst part."

Dean groaned. "Don't be so dramatic." He didn't need to ask his friend what "the worst part" was. Ronan would be happy to hold up both sides of the conversation all by himself.

"The worst part is, I'm likely to be there when she gets you killed, which means she's going to get *me* killed too."

"Oh, *that's* the problem."

"It surely is. This won't end well. Don't say I didn't warn you."

"Wouldn't dream of it," Dean said. He sat on his surfboard, bobbing along on the waves and keeping his eyes on Waverly. "Speaking of dreams," Dean grinned, "you think this place is everything she dreamed it would be?"

Ronan gripped his own surfboard tightly. "I don't care if it is or not. We shouldn't be here. We should never have come here to begin with!"

"All right," Dean said. "Calm down, I'm only kidding. I agree it's time to go."

Dean could tell Ronan was about to blow his top, and he wanted no part of that. Ronan wore his heart on his sleeve, but that sleeve also included (down near the end) a large fist Ronan used to make his point whenever words failed him. Dean had been threatened with Ronan's fist many times, and even felt it crunch his nose on one occasion. That was back before he and Ronan had become such good friends—but Dean didn't want to push his luck. Ronan was as big as a house, and Dean liked his nose the way it was. He took a long last look at the beach and sighed. "You have to admit, it's quite a sight."

"Aye, and if we linger too long, it'll be the last thing we ever see."

The two boys were floating off the coast of St. Blanc, a tiny, unspoiled island in the Caribbean Sea. An endless stretch of white sand went on for miles with nary a rock, pebble, or twig to be found. Crystal clear water sparkled where the ocean met the land, as if diamonds had been scattered in the surf.

It was late in the afternoon, and the sun was sinking down toward the sea. The sunlight laid down a golden streak toward the horizon, as if charting a course to paradise. Dean felt like he was already there. He might have wondered why anyone would leave this place, if he didn't already know the answer. He knew the stories. He knew why no one ever came to St. Blanc. Dean and his friends had been lucky so far, but the smart move would be to quit while they were ahead. Convincing Waverly of that was going to take something of an effort.

Waverly Kray was within shouting distance of Dean and Ronan, surfing a nearby wave. Ronan had been trying to call her in for ten minutes now, but she couldn't hear him. Either that or she had pretended not to. In the end, Dean and Ronan were forced to paddle out and get her.

Dean didn't mind all that much. On the way out, he marveled at the way Waverly commanded the ocean on her board, surfing inside the curl of a massive wave. The wave began to chase her as it collapsed, but Waverly crouched down low and put a hand out, grazing the surface of the water as she maintained her lead on the break. Dean watched her ride up to the crest and make a sharp turn back into the heart of the crashing wave.

Water sprayed out from the wave's lip as Waverly turned on it. She quickly swerved around again to continue streaking ahead of the curl. The cutback turn was a simple move for Dean to execute on his wheelboard, but it required one very important ingredient.

Land. In the water, Waverly turned the move into something special. She did it with a kind of slashing elegance and seemed to move in slow motion, her silhouette backlit by the sun.

"She's something else, isn't she?"

Ronan let out a terse laugh. "I'll grant you that, Seaborne."

Waverly rode her wave to the end and dove into the water, another liquid mountain conquered. She climbed back onto her board, brushed a few wet locks of auburn hair out of her face, and shook away the rest. She looked exhilarated. It made Dean happy to see her that way. He had never known a girl like Waverly before. Growing up as he had—raised by pirates, stowing away on ships, and lying to everyone he met—he had never had the opportunity. Dean counted himself lucky to have Waverly in his life, even if he did sometimes wonder if she had some kind of death wish. An old sea dog had once warned Dean that when it came to girls, the pretty ones were always a little crazy. Waverly's tanned skin, soft features, and emerald eyes covered the first part of that statement. The way she attacked waves big enough to snap a man's neck proved the rest true. She spotted Dean and Ronan and paddled over.

"Having fun, Princess?" Ronan asked.

Waverly splashed water at him. She hated being called Princess and he knew it. Her distaste for the word had only grown since it had become her rightful title. But at that moment, her spirits would not be dampened by a little friendly teasing. "The waves here are perfect! Are you two ready to give it another go?"

Dean shook his head. "Sun's getting low. We have to head back in. Now."

"Why?"

"You know why. It's not safe."

Waverly groaned. "You sound like my father. Just a little while longer. Please? I can teach you. There's no better place to learn to surf."

Before anyone could argue, a monstrous roar ripped through the air. All eyes turned down the beach, toward a wild animal in the shape of a man, only much bigger and hairier. Seconds later, a whole pack of them burst out from the trees at the end of the shoreline.

"The Parkoors might disagree with you," Ronan said.

Waverly's smile vanished. "That's them?"

Dean's face turned grim. He nodded. The creatures were giant gorillas with black pelts and white, skull-like faces—*and*, according to the French explorer who first discovered this island, extraordinary athleticism and razor-sharp claws. Dean couldn't verify that last part at his present distance, and he had no desire to get close enough to find out.

"I told you," Ronan said as the animals tore down the beach. "I told you!"

Dean heard Waverly take in a short breath. When he turned to reassure her, she was already gone. "What are you two waiting for?" she called back. "Paddle!"

"Brilliant!" Ronan said with no small amount of sarcasm as he and Dean turned their boards around to follow Waverly.

The three of them lay flat on their stomachs and paddled hard for shore on their surfboards. By the time they made it to dry land, the Parkoors were closing in on their position. The beasts moved across the sand like galloping horses, charging on all fours. Dean, Ronan, and Waverly abandoned their boards and ran for their lives.

"I told you this was a bad idea!" Ronan barked, smacking Dean in the shoulder.

"Not now!" Dean said, running hard for the trees.

"Down!" Waverly called out as the animals threw rocks at their backs.

Dean dove into the sand as stones sailed overhead as if shot from a cannon. "These things are smarter than they look."

Once the rocks stopped flying, Ronan shouted: "Go!"

"Wait!" Waverly said. "The packs!"

She doubled back and grabbed the three backpacks they had taken with them from their ship. She tossed one each to Dean and Ronan. "Just in case." The three of them ran into the jungle at the edge of the beach, as unlikely a trio as there had ever been—a pirate, a spy, and a princess. At least, those were the lives they had left behind.

Three months had passed since they had set sail together from Zenhala, the island where gold grew on trees. Three months since Dean's life had changed forever. He had gone to Zenhala as a reluctant spy for One-Eyed Jack, the Pirate King of the Caribbean. Dean had been sent to steal the island's fabled golden harvest, and he would have succeeded, too, had his heart been in the job. In the end, Dean followed his heart elsewhere. He relinquished any claim he had on the priceless treasure and left with something more valuable. Freedom. He had been denied it all the days of his criminal life, but those days were done.

Dean also left Zenhala with the first real friends he had ever known. There was Ronan, who had come to help Dean steal the island's treasure, and Waverly, a noble girl of thirteen who had more in common with a couple of reformed pirates than she did her fellow blue bloods. Together, they struck off in search of adventure and the chance to chart their own course in life. It had been Waverly's idea to make the trip to St. Blanc—"the world's most perfect beach." Dean had known the risks going in, but he had a hard time saying no to Waverly.

Ronan didn't have the same weakness where Waverly was concerned. He had argued strongly against making the trip to St. Blanc. He had worried about the island's proximity to waters controlled by the English navy, though that was true of almost everywhere in the Caribbean, now that One-Eyed Jack was gone. With a little help from a sea serpent who lived off the coast of Zenhala, Dean had seen the cutthroat captain off to Davy Jones's Locker. But mostly, Ronan had worried about the Parkoors.

Dean, Ronan, and Waverly fought their way through a tangled web of tropical vegetation, trying to put some distance between themselves and the wild animals behind them. The dense thicket slowed them down considerably, but it had the opposite effect on their simian pursuers. Dean noticed a complex network of vines in the trees overhead. The vines crisscrossed throughout the jungle canopy, strung from branch to branch. In a flash, the Parkoors caught up to the trio. One of the Parkoors dropped out of the trees, right in Dean and Ronan's path.

Running too fast to stop, Ronan barreled into the creature. He sandwiched the Parkoor against a palm tree and knocked its head hard against the trunk. Dean slid toward them feet first, taking out the Parkoor's legs before it could take out Ronan. They hit the dirt in a tangled mess. Dean rolled hard to the right as the gorilla growled and took a swipe at him. Its nails tore his shirt, cutting his skin.

Razor-sharp claws. Check.

He got up quickly as Waverly tossed something his way.

"What am I supposed to do with a coconut?"

"What do you think? Hit him!"

Dean clocked the beast in the head hard enough to break the coconut apart. The Parkoor's eyes rolled up toward the back of its head, and the creature went to sleep. "That's one down," Dean said, helping Ronan up.

Ronan looked back the other way. "We're going to need a lot

more coconuts." Another wave of Parkoors bounded through the trees, hard and fast. They danced across the vines and jumped off tree branches, launching themselves forward.

"This way," Waverly pointed. "Up the mountain."

"That's why you grabbed the packs," Ronan grumbled. "You still want to make that jump."

Waverly nodded. "If it keeps us alive. Come on!" She ran for the rocks up ahead. Dean and Ronan followed. What else could they do?

Mont Blanc stood five hundred feet tall, right in the center of the island. It rose up out of the jungle to a barren peak that overlooked the many bays and inlets of St. Blanc. A man named Verrick, one of Waverly's loyal subjects and as seasoned a sailor as Dean had ever known, had their ship waiting in one of those bays.

The Parkoors continued to gain ground as Dean and his friends scrambled up the mountain. The animals were superior climbers by far, but Dean, Waverly, and Ronan had the high ground and used it to their advantage. As soon as they reached a stable plateau, they stopped to throw rocks back the other way. Ronan had an arm like a cannon and threw hard enough to puncture a ship's hull. The relentless Parkoors flew up the mountain like leaping spiders, but Ronan picked them off with stones and sent them tumbling back down.

Waverly reached the mountaintop first, with Dean and Ronan close behind. As mountains went, Mont Blanc was rather small, but it boasted a spectacular view from the summit just the same. The three friends stopped to catch their breath on a rocky crag overlooking the island. "It really is beautiful here," Waverly remarked. "Imagine what it'll look like on the way down."

Dean tugged on the straps of his pack. "You're sure these will work?"

"I packed them myself," Waverly assured him. "They'll work."

"I don't like this," Ronan said.

"Have you got a better idea?" Waverly asked.

"No," Ronan answered grudgingly.

Waverly stifled a laugh. "Then I'm heading for the ship." She backed up a few paces, then ran full bore at the edge of the mountain. When she jumped, she let out a gleeful howl.

Dean shook his head. *Just like the old man said. Crazy.*

He watched as a folded shroud of silk flew out of Waverly's backpack and opened up with a loud whomp. It caught the wind like a sail, and she drifted down to safety. Ronan shook his head. "I can't do this."

"No choice," Dean said, looking out for the Parkoors. They were still coming up the mountain. "Time's wasting."

Ronan didn't budge. "You go first."

Dean studied Ronan. He had never known his friend to be afraid of anything, but the look in Ronan's eyes told Dean he'd rather face the Parkoors than the cliff. "I'm not going to jump until you do, Ronan. Get to it."

Ronan refused. He was scared of the leap. So was Dean, but the thought of getting torn limb from limb by a family of wild gorillas scared him more. Grunting and growling sounds drifted up the mountain path.

Dean grabbed Ronan and shook him. "You hear that? Now *you're* the one who's going to get us killed. Come on, Ronan! Jump!"

The Parkoors came into view, and Ronan came to his senses. He cursed Dean under his breath as he backed up from the ledge and got ready to jump. A moment later, he was in the air, gliding along like a child strapped to a giant kite. It was Dean's turn next. He got a running start and leaped, just as his friends had done.

But it was too late. The Parkoors had reached the summit. One of them tackled Dean in midair. They plunged through the sky, grappling at each other. Dean kicked the beast off and prayed that its claws had not torn the fabric inside his pack. If he wanted to live, he had two seconds to release the portable sail he carried.

It took him three.

CHAPTER 2

JUNGLE HUNT

The straps of Dean's pack dug in underneath his arms. His body jerked upward as the silk canopy flapped open, but his feet were already nearing the treetops. The last thing Dean saw before he reentered the jungle was a ship approaching St. Blanc. It was headed for the same sheltered bay that harbored Verrick and their ship, the *Tideturner*.

The next thing Dean saw was an extreme close-up of palm leaves, vines, and tree bark. Dean bounced through the foliage, hitting branch after painful branch all the way down. Everything went black, and for a moment, Dean's world ceased to exist.

• • •

Dean woke up with his feet dangling in the air. His lines and rigging had gotten caught in the trees, and he was swinging from a branch like a wind chime. He rubbed his aching head and took stock of his situation. Judging from the position of the sun in the sky, he hadn't been out for very long. He slipped out of his pack and climbed down to the ground.

Dean's stomach tightened up when he heard more Parkoors in the distance. He had to keep moving. Verrick had the *Tideturner* in a cove not far from where he stood. Dean knew that. He had seen it. He just had to get there. Waverly and Ronan would be waiting for him on board the ship, assuming they didn't think he was already dead.

No, Dean thought. He refused to believe his friends would leave him. They would be there with Verrick. He just had to clear the jungle before the sun went down.

Dean pressed on through the leafy green labyrinth. He got turned around more than once. His head was pounding, and the jungle faded in and out of focus. He realized he must have hit his head harder than he thought. Dean needed to rest, but he couldn't afford to stop moving. Soon everything was spinning. He took a break and steadied himself against a tree. No use—he was ready to collapse when at last he heard the waves lapping against the bay shore.

A burst of energy surged into Dean's legs, and he stumbled through an opening in the trees to emerge safely on the opposite end of the island. He fell to his knees and closed his eyes. The ship was there. He had made it. He could relax.

The hammers cocked on a dozen rifles, and Dean blinked his eyes open. The ship in the bay was not the *Tideturner*. The flag it flew was the Union Jack, and Dean's friends were nowhere to be found. In their place, he saw a contingent of English sailors with their muskets locked and loaded. Off to the side stood their captain, resplendent in his crisp blue-and-white uniform.

"Stay there, if you please."

Dean put his hands up. He said nothing.

The captain motioned for one of his men to inspect Dean. "See if he's our man. Or boy, as the case may be."

The sailor checked the inside of Dean's left arm and found a tattoo in the shape of three wave crests rising inside a circle. One-Eyed Jack had branded him with the mark long ago.

"It's him," said the sailor.

A superior smile formed on the captain's lips. "Dean Seaborne. Last of the pirate king's spies. Young sir, you are under arrest."

CHAPTER 3

THE DOCK OF THE BAY

"All rise!"

The court officer's booming voice echoed through the room. Everyone present got up on their feet at his command, but not Dean. He was already standing in the dock.

"The court will now hear the matter of the Crown versus Dean Seaborne, the Right Honorable Lord Justice Wellington presiding."

A large old man wearing red robes with black trim ambled into the courtroom and took his seat at the bench. The judge had bags under his eyes and thick, rubbery jowls that made him look like a hound dog in a powdered wig. He exhaled loudly as he sat down and the rest of his legal entourage filed in. He was followed by the chairman of the court and the mayor of Port Royal, an English harbor on the island of Jamaica, where Dean had been taken for his trial. The mayor had no power in the courtroom, but he had been granted a seat on the bench as a courtesy, which was the custom. Also there to assist the Lord Justice were two local magistrates and two barristers, one for the prosecution and the other for the defense. Dean didn't know any of them. He just knew the court had gotten a lot of people out of bed that morning to hang little old him.

The jury came in last. Twelve good men and true, as Dean had heard people say. He wished he had a friend among their number. Dean's only friends were up in the gallery, along with the other people who had come to watch the show.

Ronan and Waverly sat in the front row, sporting guilt-ridden faces. Verrick sat with them. He was an older gentleman with a full head of stark white hair and a short, thick beard. With his caring, grandfatherly face, Verrick mouthed the words, *Steady on*, and offered Dean a reassuring nod. Waverly and Ronan attempted similar looks of encouragement. Dean forced a thin smile for them, but there was no hope behind it. Not in this place. Port Royal had once been a thriving pirate stronghold, but the English had since turned it into a place of execution.

Dean envied Ronan's spot in the gallery. Ronan had been a pirate too, but he had done his dirty work with the Pirate Youth. None of their victims had ever spoken a word to anyone about their raids. The sailors on the ships that Ronan's crew hit were always too embarrassed to admit they had been bested by a crew made up of children. Dean, on the other hand, could not hide who he had been. He looked down at the triple-wave tattoo on the inside of his left arm.

The mark had served many purposes. Its presence on Dean's arm had meant that he could stand before any pirate in One-Eyed Jack's Black Fleet and identify himself as one of their own. It had also meant Dean could be more easily spotted and tracked if he ever tried to escape his sworn duty to One-Eyed Jack. The cursed mark had hounded Dean while One-Eyed Jack was still alive and continued to do so even after the man's death.

The world was not a safe place for pirates anymore. Shortly after One-Eyed Jack had gotten himself swallowed up by that sea serpent, the surviving members of his Black Fleet started fighting over who should inherit the mantle of leadership. In the end, no one did. The pirates' infighting made them easy pickings for agents of the Crown, and the English navy rounded up most of the Black Fleet when it took their stronghold at Bartleby Bay. The navy didn't stop there, either. It recovered One-Eyed Jack's black book, a list of every pirate who had ever signed into his service, and went to work crossing off names. Spies like Dean became marked men in more ways than one, as the English made their push to clean up the waters of the Caribbean.

Lord Justice Wellington cleared his throat. When he coughed, it sounded like he had a pound of seaweed in his gullet. "Dean Seaborne," he croaked, "you stand accused of piracy, a most heinous crime. How do you plead?"

Dean squirmed in his little wooden pen, wondering how best to answer the judge's question. *Guilty, but it wasn't my fault? Guilty, but with a good explanation?* That wouldn't do. He looked to his barrister. The man who was there to represent Dean said nothing. He was a distracted, disinterested fellow whose name Dean had already forgotten. Dean had met him briefly before the trial, and the encounter had done nothing to boost his spirits. His barrister looked like he had been out all night carousing, and had nodded off twice while they discussed his defense. Dean was on his own.

"I'm innocent, your honor," Dean said.

The judge aimed a knowing smile at the Crown prosecutor. Dean got the sense that neither man had ever heard a pirate claim otherwise. The prosecutor stifled a laugh, as did the two local magistrates on the bench. A few members of the jury even tittered along with them.

So much for a fair trial, thought Dean.

"The Crown may call its first witness," said the judge.

The prosecutor rose from his seat. He was a serious man, the polar opposite of his counterpart. "May it please the court, the Crown calls Captain Wallace Grimmault."

Dean looked around the courtroom. He didn't recognize the name, but the face of the man who climbed into the witness stand was familiar. Dean's stomach turned cold as the man placed what had once been his right hand on the Bible and swore that the testimony he gave the court would be the truth. The prosecutor apologized and instructed Grimmault to repeat the gesture with his intact left hand. Dean was sure the misunderstanding had been rehearsed, but he found it no less effective for that.

"Please state your name for the record," said the prosecutor.

"Wallace Grimmault," said the witness.

"Not *Captain* Wallace Grimmault?"

The witness shook his head. "No sir. Not anymore."

Grimmault was a slight man, thinner than Dean remembered. Most of the former captain's face disappeared behind a bushy brown beard that was flecked with gray, but his eyes stood out. They simmered with anger. Wallace Grimmault had combed his short hair neatly and put on his finest clothes, which were not very fine. He was a poor man who had fallen on hard times, and Dean knew exactly when they had begun.

"Do you know the accused?" asked the prosecutor, motioning to Dean.

Grimmault tilted his head. "That depends."

The prosecutor turned. "I'm sorry?"

"I don't know anyone called Dean Seaborne, but I do know the boy standing in the dock."

The prosecutor feigned confusion. "I'm afraid I don't understand. Please explain."

"He came aboard my ship as a cabin boy, two years ago. Presented himself as a Master Tom Hawkins." Grimmault shrugged. "Seemed a nice enough lad. Hard worker, did his duties ably. Everyone liked him. Wasn't long before he knew everything there was to know about the *Audrey May*. That was my ship, you see. We made three trips with him on board without any problems. Just minor shipments here in the islands. Nothing of any great value. That all changed when we were engaged to transport Lord Giles Nedley and his family on holiday."

The prosecutor put on a concerned face. "What happened then?"

"Pirates," Grimmault said. "Sunk us off the coast of Tortuga. Took Lord Nedley and his family hostage."

"I remember this story," said the prosecutor. "If I'm not mistaken, Lord Nedley and his family were ransomed back to their relations in London at a considerable cost."

"Aye, sir. We all paid a price that day." Grimmault held up his hook. "For some of us, no amount of money can bring back what we lost."

Grimmault lowered his hand and stared at Dean, who found it impossible to meet the man's gaze.

"And you believe that this boy was a willing accomplice of the pirates who attacked you?" the prosecutor asked Grimmault.

"I know he was."

The Crown prosecutor put a finger to his lips, as if considering the idea for the first time. "Forgive me, sir. You've been through a terrible ordeal and you have my sympathy, but how can you be sure? What proof do you have that Dean Seaborne was at the heart of this vile scheme?"

"I was there!" Grimmault thundered. "I saw! The pirate captain spared him. Only him. He checked the mark on the lad's arm and recognized him as one of his confederates. He took him with the hostages and left the rest of us to drown. Was luck alone that saved our lives, as another ship passed through soon after."

A dreadful murmur ran through the jury. Satisfied, the prosecutor returned to his seat. "No further questions, your honor."

"Cross-examination?" the judge asked lazily.

He received no reply from Dean's counsel.

The judge gave an impatient, attention-seeking cough. More seaweed phlegm that would never be dredged up from his throat. But he succeeded in catching the eye of Dean's representative.

"Hmn?" Dean's lawyer asked. "No, thank you. No questions, your honor." He spoke with the air of a man politely declining a tray of cakes at tea.

"No questions?" Dean blurted out. "You're not going to ask him anything?"

Another rumbling cough poured out of the judge. "The defendant is instructed not to speak unless spoken to. Your barrister will speak for you."

"But he's not saying anything," Dean protested.

Dean's barrister poked a spot of crust from his eye. "What's that?"

"Tell them what I told you! I was there against my will."

Dean's barrister fought back a yawn. "I can't tell the witness anything. I'm only empowered to ask questions."

"Then ask him! What makes him think I was a willing accomplice?"

The judge banged his gavel. "The defendant will be silent."

Grimmault pointed his hook at Dean. "You held up that tattoo and identified yourself as One-Eyed Jack's man. Do you deny it?"

Dean shook his head. "You don't understand. I was forced into that life."

"Then it's true," the Crown prosecutor observed. "You were there as a spy."

"A-ha!" Grimmault said. "He admits it!"

"Objection!" Dean called out.

"Order! Order in the court!" The judge pounded his gavel hard enough to splinter the wood. "The defendant will be silent or the sergeant-at-mace will see that he is removed!"

"But—"

"One more word, young man—one more!—and I will hold you in contempt! Do you wish to be tried in absentia?"

Dean held his tongue. He didn't know where absentia was, but he had no desire to find out. The judge continued his reprimand.

"You will be afforded the opportunity to make a statement in your defense at the end of the trial. Until then? Keep. Your. Mouth. Shut. Am I clear?"

"Yes, your honor," Dean said, sufficiently chastened.

"Next witness!" shouted the judge.

Dean sighed as another witness took the stand to tell the world of his crimes. One after the other, familiar faces appeared to recount the horrors that had been done to them at the hands of One-Eyed Jack's men.

There were people who had lost everything:

We had planned to start a new life in the colonies. We were so happy and full of hope. That all ended the day the pirates sacked our ship.

There were people who had been marooned:

The buccaneers left us on an island no bigger than this room. Left us with nothing! Not even a drop of water!

There were people who had lost their loved ones:

My husband was on board the H.M.S. Adventure *when it went down. Not a day goes by that I don't miss him and curse the pirates who took him from us. Because of them, my son will never know his father!*

Dean's heart sank a little further with each weepy tale of woe. They were all terrible, and all true. He wished it were otherwise, but the part he played in each sad story was undeniable. In every case, he had been the one who had made the raid possible. He had been the one sent to find out the ship's cargo, where it was going, and when. He had identified the most profitable moment to strike and relayed that information to One-Eyed Jack's Black Fleet.

Without any cross-examination of the witnesses, whether Dean had a choice in the matter never came up. He had been raised by pirates, and that life was all he had known. Dean had once tried to escape his profession and nearly got fed to a family of sharks for his trouble, but no one asked about that. Meanwhile, his barrister openly snored.

As the trial wore on, no contrast emerged to the picture being painted of Dean as a heartless pirate spy. It would've been a hard point to argue, even if the judge had allowed Dean to make the argument. The witnesses' testimony hit him as hard as anyone. He remembered every raid the witnesses mentioned, but it was one thing to know about a crime. It was quite another to learn the human cost of it.

Dean had never known what became of the Black Fleet's victims after the fighting was over. Those details would stick with him now, as would the faces of the grieving widows and teary-eyed children in court. He could only imagine what the jury thought of him. And Waverly . . . she turned greener around the gills with each heartbreaking story. Eventually, she could listen to no more and hurried out of the courtroom. Verrick followed, her dutiful guardian.

Dean braced himself for the next witness, but at long last, the prosecutor declined to call one. Having built a strong (if not unassailable) case against Dean, he stated, "The prosecution rests, your honor."

Dean was still looking at the door that Waverly had left through when he heard his barrister mumble, "The defense also rests."

"What?" Dean's head whipped around. "No, we don't!"

The bumbling barrister leaned forward with his elbows on the table before him. "Yes, rest," he said, massaging his temples. "Oh, I need rest."

"Your honor," Dean said, "I haven't had a chance to speak."

Dean's plea met with the familiar rapping of a gavel. "The defense has rested," said the judge. "If it was your intention to speak, you should have arranged that with your representative before now."

"You're not serious," Dean said. "Of course I wanted to speak. I told you that! You said I'd get the chance to make a statement!"

"It is not the responsibility of this court to manage your defense strategy."

"Strategy? What strategy? Look at him!" Dean thrust both hands at the wastrel assigned to speak in his defense. The judge was unmoved. "This trial is a farce!" Dean spat. "A travesty!"

The court members gasped.

"What did you say?" coughed the judge, clearly rattled.

"You heard me," Dean scowled. Rage bubbled up inside of him. He knew he was crossing a line, but he couldn't stop himself. He was on trial for his life, and the game was rigged. "You're not even giving me a chance! What am I doing here if you won't let me defend myself?"

"Have it your way, young man." The judge gave a nod to the sergeant-at-mace, a stone-faced wall of a man who carried an actual mace. He grabbed Dean and pulled him from the dock.

"No!" Dean shouted as he was forcibly removed from the courtroom. "This isn't fair! It's not fair!"

Dean protested his ejection all the way out the door, but it gained him nothing. He was not allowed back into court until it was time for the jury to read the verdict. They took less than five minutes to find him guilty as charged.

CHAPTER 4

Just Passing Through

Lord Justice Wellington was surprisingly lenient when it came time for Dean's sentencing. He must have had a soft spot in his heart for children, because he overlooked the tantrum Dean had thrown at the end of his trial and handed down the merciful sentence of ninety-five years in prison. At first, Dean didn't appreciate what a gift he'd been given, but the judge explained how this was all for Dean's betterment as a person. He reminded Dean that death was the standard punishment for pirates and suggested that he look on the bright side of things.

"In addition to avoiding the hangman's noose, I'm granting you the opportunity to shave years off your sentence. All it takes is good behavior. If you prove to be a model inmate, you could be a free man in just ..." The judge paused to do some quick math at the bench. "Eighty-two years!"

Everyone appeared to be pleased with the verdict, except for Ronan and three rough-looking men in the back row. Dean hadn't noticed them before, but they stood out to him now. There was a dreadlocked Jamaican, a towering man who could barely squeeze into his seat, and a third man who stood out simply by being ugly as sin. They had cleaned up as best they could, but Dean knew pirates when he saw them. The question was, what were they doing here? If Dean were one of them, he wouldn't come near this island, let alone its courtroom.

As the sergeant-at-mace walked Dean out of court, Ronan stood up and shouted after him. "This isn't over, Seaborne! We'll figure something out, you hear me? Don't give up hope!"

Ronan's message was wasted on Dean. It would take more than words to help him now. The lockup was right next door to the courthouse. Dean was remanded into custody, and a pair of guards marched him up to the second floor of the prison. They removed his shackles, threw him in a cell, and slammed the door. That was it. His short life as a free man was over.

Dean rubbed his wrists and took a look at his new accommodations. The holding cell was large, and he was not alone in it. A handful of pirates milled about in the center of the room, standing in the light of a lone window. More convicts lined the walls, either preferring the shadows or lacking the energy to leave them. The heat in the cell was oppressive. The muggy air reeked of body odor and other smells Dean preferred not to investigate. Unless the powers that be opted to transfer him to Newgate Prison in London, this would likely be his home for the next ninety-five years.

The thought turned Dean's stomach. Everything he had ever heard about Newgate was a nightmare, but he found himself hoping for a transfer just the same. If nothing else, the move might present him with an opportunity to escape.

Escape.

That was the dream Dean would have to cling to now if he wanted to survive. Ronan had been right—to keep going required hope. Unfortunately, Dean saw little reason to hope for anything in this place. Large stones formed the walls, mortared together with thick cement. Strong iron bars penned the prisoners in, keeping them in full view of the guards at all times.

Dean put on a brave face and walked to the window. Outside, in the streets of Port Royal, the world was going on without him. "I gave up the throne of Zenhala for this?" he asked himself. At the moment, the freedom to chart his own course in life felt vastly overrated.

"Move!" someone shouted. Dean jumped, but the order wasn't meant for him. He turned and saw his jailers ushering another prisoner into the cell. Dean recognized him as the ugly man he had just seen in court. *Captured already?* He shook his head as the guards urged the man forward.

"I'm moving, I'm moving," said the man. "A little patience might be in order. Ain't easy takin' the stairs on one leg."

Dean looked closer. Sure enough, the man was struggling along on top of one peg leg and a crutch. When at last he reached the threshold of the cell, the guards took his crutch away.

"I'll be needing that," the man said.

The guard with the crutch shook his head. "Can't take anything in there that might be used as a weapon."

"That ain't no weapon, it's me crutch. I need it to walk!"

"You're in luck, then," the guard laughed. "There's nowhere to go. Have a seat."

"Don't worry, we'll give it back when you walk to the gallows," the other guard chimed in. They both found the situation very funny.

The ugly man snarled as they shut him in. "It's a wicked thing, taking a crippled man's crutch. A wicked thing indeed!" He looked around at his fellow prisoners. "Who'll give an old buccaneer a hand? You there, boy! Help me to that window."

Dean sighed. He wanted to be left alone, but in prison, there was safety in numbers. Dean knew he was better off with a friend to stand beside him, even if they did only have three legs between the two of them. And he couldn't leave a one-legged man to hobble across the room by himself. Not when the man was asking for help.

Dean put his shoulder under the man's arm, taking the place of his missing crutch. The man put no weight at all on his peg leg as they staggered across the cell together. He was heavy, but Dean managed. "There's a good lad. Thank you kindly." Dean grunted as they reached the window and sat down with their backs to the wall.

The man let out a deep breath and massaged the stump of his amputated leg. "Thanks again, lad."

"Don't mention it. That wasn't right what they did, taking your crutch."

"Ain't that the truth?" The man spit on the floor and gave the guards the evil eye. They were too busy playing cards to notice. "Don't matter, though. All's well now. I'm right where I want to be."

The man leaned back with a smile on his face, but what he had to be happy about, Dean could not hope to guess. He looked like he'd been hit in the face with a frying pan—crooked brown teeth and a nose like a potato. Sharp cheekbones and a protruding brow surrounded a pair of scheming eyes. Dean had judged the man ugly from a distance, but up close, he was a gargoyle.

"If this is where you *want* to be, you need to raise your standards," Dean said.

"Hah!" the man laughed. "The boy's a quick one. Pleased ta meet ya, lad. Alec Skinner, at yer service. Captain Alec Skinner."

The captain offered his hand, and Dean shook it.

"Dean Seaborne."

"I know. I was there in court today, listenin' to every word. That's quite a body of work you've put together. Very impressive for a boy your age."

Dean frowned. "I'm not proud of it."

"Course not," Skinner said. "They left out yer crowning achievement!" He leaned in to whisper, "The way I hear it, you're the spy what led the Black Fleet to Zenhala."

The mention of Zenhala stopped Dean cold. He made a point of never talking about the island with anyone but Ronan, Verrick, and Waverly. There was a secret to finding the Golden Isle, one that every pirate in the Caribbean would've killed to learn. "You don't really believe that story . . ."

Skinner rubbed his beard. "Enough pirates say it, a man gets to wondering. Way I heard it, the Black Fleet looted that island and left with a boat full of golden trees—the haul of a lifetime— but came back here with nothing. Less than nothing! Not even One-Eyed Jack. How do ya suppose that happened?"

Dean shrugged. "He probably went down in the storm. Either that or he kept the golden harvest for himself. He was never big on sharing."

"No." Skinner shook his head with a laugh. "Speaking from my own personal experience, he was not. I haven't sailed the Caribbean in ten years 'cause of him. Couldn't work an inch of these waters, all 'cause I refused to bend my knee to the great Pirate King."

Dean raised an eyebrow. "You weren't one of One-Eyed Jack's men?"

Skinner scrunched up his face. "Lord, no! You won't find me

shedding one salty tear for that old blackguard. Good riddance, I say!" He spat again. "I made my bones workin' for me own self, raiding ships in places you ain't never heard of."

Dean blinked. "So what brought you here?"

Skinner grinned a crook-toothed grin. "I'm here for the same reason I went to court today. The same reason I'm sittin' in this cell. I'm here for you, Dean Seaborne."

"For me? Why?"

"Got a proposition for you, lad." He jerked a thumb toward the guards and their card game. "You think these numbskulls caught me? Not a chance. I turned myself in after you got sentenced. Had to make sure you and I got a proper chance to talk."

"About what?" Dean said, afraid that he already knew the answer. "I can't take you to Zenhala, if that's what you're after."

"I'm not here for that."

"What, then?"

Skinner nodded toward their cellmates with a disapproving look. "I'd prefer to have the conversation elsewhere."

"I don't think we have a choice."

Skinner unscrewed his peg leg and took out a stick of dynamite that he had hidden inside. "Don't we, though?"

CHAPTER 5

DECISIONS

Dean plugged his ears and closed his eyes.

The explosion blasted a hole in the base of the wall, creating a crack that ran up to the window. The opening wasn't big enough to squeeze through, but it would be soon enough.

"Have at it, boys!" Skinner shouted, pointing at the break in the wall.

After the blast, the guards took more of an interest in what was happening inside the cell. One of them called downstairs for backup and the other fiddled with his key ring, trying to fit the right key into the lock. Meanwhile, every able-bodied man in the lockup threw his shoulder into the wall. The prisoners attacked the breach like human battering rams and quickly broke through.

"Stop!" the guards shouted, as a dozen pirates rushed to freedom. Dean was about to follow them out when Skinner grabbed him by the shoulder.

"Ease up a point there, lad. Good things come to those who wait."

Sure enough, when the guards finally opened the cell door, every one of them began chasing after the escaped pirates. Dean and the sly captain waited until the last guard went out through the wall, leaving the prison empty. Skinner motioned to the cell door, which, in their haste, the guards had neglected to close.

"Shall we?"

Dean picked Skinner's crutch up off the floor. "I think this belongs to you."

Once outside, Dean and Skinner started down a narrow street, keeping off the main roads. They walked with purpose, trying not to draw attention as they moved away from the wild gang of pirates running in the opposite direction, soon to be recaptured.

"I need to find my friends," Dean said.

"Already taken care of," Skinner replied. "Told my men ta find that boy who called out to ya in court. They'll have yer ship waitin' at Gallows Point, as per me orders."

"Gallows Point? That's where they hang the prisoners on this island."

"One of me better ideas. What's the last place *you'd* expect a couple 'a' fugitive pirates to run to after a jailbreak?"

"Fair point," Dean said. "Except I'm not a pirate anymore."

"Sorry, laddie," Skinner laughed. "You don't get to make that decision."

Dean followed Skinner through Port Royal, keeping a sharp lookout for the authorities. They stuck to busy market streets in the nicer parts of town, avoiding the slums most pirates would run to. Skinner was a smart one, Dean could tell, but he also knew the man's help came at a price.

"You busted me out for a reason," Dean said. "Let's hear it."

"One word," Skinner said as they neared the docks at Gallows Point. "Aquatica."

"Aquatica?" Dean stopped short, unable to hide his surprise.

"You've heard of it. Good. What do you say? Fancy a trip? You and yer friends?"

Dean trained a cynical eye on Skinner. "There's no such place."

"Know that for a fact, do ya?"

Dean shrugged. "I hear stories, same as anyone. I don't always believe them . . ."

"Humor me, lad," Skinner said. "Ya owe me that much, I think."

"It's supposed to be some kind of retreat," Dean said. "A private island for royals on holiday."

"Not exclusive to royalty. It's just the cost ta spend a night there is so expensive, only nobles can afford ta pay it. And it's not an island, either. It's a castle. A fortress-at-sea."

"As far as I know, it's a fish story. A con that pirates use on wealthy marks they mean to rob and maroon."

"Seems ta me, folks said the same thing about Zenhala."

Dean looked away. Skinner had a point.

"I seen it with me own eyes." Skinner raised his right hand in the air, as if to swear on the fact. "Just south of Trinidad and the Tobago Cays. It's *real*."

Dean studied Skinner's ugly face. "Say it is real. Why tell me?"

"Yer a smart lad. I'm sure you can piece together your part in this."

Dean frowned. "You need a spy."

Skinner nodded. "I don't have a fleet 'a' pirate ships ta help me storm the castle. I need a savvy mate ta go in first. Lower the defenses. Raise the gates. Spent a lotta time tryin' ta find the right man fer the job. When I heard about a boy who led the Black Fleet to Zenhala, I told my crew, that's just the kind of spy we need."

They had reached the docks. Dean spotted the *Tideturner* moored at the end of a pier. He wanted off this island and out of this conversation.

"Captain Skinner, listen, I—"

"Don't answer straight away," Skinner said, cutting Dean off. "Give it a good think. A tropical island resort that caters to the world's most exclusive clientele . . . a lavish and lively court filled with decadent luxuries . . . wonders and riches from all around the world! It's the score of a lifetime, and you'll find I share the wealth a lot better than One-Eyed Jack."

Skinner waited for Dean's eyes to light up at the promise of loot. Once he realized it wasn't going to happen, he took another tack. "I can see yer not one ta make hasty decisions. That's fair enough—ya don't know me from Adam. Can I ask that we at least board this here ship and go on talkin' below deck? We need to step lively before we get hauled back ta prison, and I've gone as far as I can on one bad leg an' a crutch."

Dean sighed. He had hoped that they might part ways here, but Skinner's mates were nowhere in sight and the *Tideturner* was the only ship ready for sea. He couldn't just leave the man standing on the dock. Not after everything he'd done. Dean brought him on board, making excuses about Aquatica the whole way.

"Captain, it's not that I don't appreciate everything you did to get me out of jail and back to my ship. I'm in your debt, truly. But, this job . . ." Dean shook his head. "I can't help you with it. I don't do that kind of thing anymore."

"Gone the high road, have ya? Not to worry. You'll come 'round ta my way of thinking."

"Not likely."

"Oh, I hope that's not true," Skinner said, as he climbed on deck with a little help from Dean. "I'd hate to have gone through all this trouble for nothin'."

Skinner made a clicking sound with his mouth, and a pair of

large hands pinned Dean's arms behind his back. He let out a yelp and tried to break away, but it was no use. He was locked in the grip of a giant.

The tall man from court, Dean realized. Skinner's henchman spun him around, and Dean saw the Jamaican was there too. Ronan, Verrick, and Waverly were all tied up beside him.

"Allow me to introduce my associates," Skinner said with a flourish of his hand. "Marlon Spyke . . ." The black man flipped a dagger in the air and caught it between two fingers.

"And this here's Tom Kincannon." Skinner reached up to slap the giant on the shoulder. "Also known as Long Tom Cannon."

Dean scowled at Skinner, who looked even uglier than he had a moment earlier. "They're my two best men. Dependin' on how you look at it, they're also my two worst. Now, fer the sake of yer friends, ya might want ta reconsider my offer."

PART TWO

ONE LAST JOB

CHAPTER 6

LET'S MAKE A DEAL

The journey to Aquatica was excruciating. Skinner confined Dean and his friends to quarters the whole way. He kept everyone in separate cabins and he did it without barring a single door. The pirate captain bound his captives with chains forged out of fear itself.

"I'm only gonna say this once," he warned Dean as he shut him in. "You set one foot outside this room, and I'll slice off yer lady friend's pinkie toes. Try to talk to one of yer friends without my say-so, and I'll cut off both her ears."

Dean's mouth fell open. "You wouldn't dare."

"Try me. I'll be tellin' yer friends the same story, and you better hope they listen. What happens next is up to you and yours, understand?" Skinner grabbed one of Dean's ears and gave it a painful turn.

Dean understood all right. Skinner had them right where he wanted them. Unable to communicate with his friends for fear of what horrors might befall them, Dean was stuck acting as his own guard. As the trip wore on, he grew mad with worry. Days later, when Skinner finally let him out of his room, Dean was almost afraid to leave.

The sun momentarily blinded Dean's eyes when he returned to the top deck of the *Tideturner*. After his vision adjusted, he saw a boat off the starboard bow. They had rendezvoused with Skinner's ship, a brigantine christened the *Crimson Tide*. A ragged band of scoundrels hung off the gunwales and rigging as they made their approach. Long Tom Cannon hailed the crew, and the rowdy scalawags hollered back. There had to be at least fifty men on board.

"Where are my friends?" Dean demanded, trying hard not to sound afraid.

"Pipe down, they're coming," Skinner replied. He was on the port side, leaning on his crutch and looking out across the ocean through a spyglass. Dean noticed he had screwed on a fresh peg leg (minus the dynamite, judging by his stance). Marlon Spyke brought Ronan up a moment later. Ronan looked like he'd been through the same emotional ringer Dean had.

"You all right?" Dean asked him.

Ronan nodded. "I'll feel better once I hit something."

"Hold that thought. We're not there yet."

Ronan grimaced at the shipful of pirates alongside them. "We better get there soon."

Waverly and Verrick came up next. A wave of relief crashed over Dean when he saw them both alive and unharmed. "There you are!" he exclaimed as he rushed to them—and then recoiled, taking stock of Verrick's haggard appearance. The old man looked dead on his feet.

"He slept with one eye open, protecting me these last few days," Waverly explained. "If he slept at all."

"They locked you up together?" Ronan asked.

"He wouldn't leave my side." Waverly put a hand on Verrick's weary shoulder. "He was very brave."

Dean felt a pang in his stomach. Waverly's royal father had sent Verrick as her chaperone when they left Zenhala, but that was just because she was heading off to sea with two teenage boys. No one had expected them to end up trapped on a ship full of pirates. They had to get away, but how?

"He shoulda' let himself get some decent shut-eye," Skinner called across the ship. "Yer fate was in yer own hands these past few days, not mine. I don't hurt people without a reason. I'm not a monster, you know."

"Says the man who kidnapped us and threatened us with dismemberment," Waverly fired back.

Skinner shrugged. "Don't take it personal, lass. It's just business."

"What business is that?" Verrick asked. "What do you want? I demand to know what this is about."

"Fair enough!" Skinner flipped his spyglass around, offering it to Verrick. "See for yourself, old-timer. It's right out there."

Verrick took the spyglass and brought it to his eye. "What am I looking at?"

"An oasis of finery and elegance in this filthy world of ours," Skinner said. "They call it Aquatica. It's a palace splendid enough to make a king and queen feel at home, with a treasure vault rich enough ta make an earl look like a pauper."

"*If* the stories are true," Dean said. He had a look next. Through the spyglass, he saw something at the edge of the horizon. It was far away and hard to make out, but it looked like a castle of some kind. Dean couldn't say for sure if it was Aquatica, but he didn't care to argue one way or the other. All he cared about was his friends. "Congratulations, you found it. Why don't you storm the castle and leave us out of it?"

"Would that I could, boy, would that I could." Skinner leaned in and raised the glass back to Dean's eye. "Look to the battlements. Cannons upon cannons upon cannons. They'd blow us outta the water before we ever got close enough ta scale the walls. I told you, I need someone to go in and lower their defenses." He gestured to the band of cutthroats on board his ship. "My men aren't suited ta that sort of work. I need someone who can get inside and catch 'em unawares. Someone they won't suspect."

"This lot ain't long on subtlety," Marlon Spyke noted.

"Not at all. As fer me . . . ," Skinner continued. He raised his chin in the air, putting his ugly mug on display. "Lord knows I got a face that folks don't trust easy. That's where you come in, Seaborne." He pinched one of Dean's soft cheeks and gave it a hearty shake. "You could play the part I need just fine. I had hoped ya might realize the potential here and sign aboard gladly. At the very least, ya mighta' done it outta gratitude fer me pullin' yer hide outta prison, but no. You had ta be thick about it." Skinner shook his head with a disappointed *tsk-tsk-tsk*. "No matter, I'm prepared for that. You'll go along as long as I've got yer friends as my guests. The journey here proved that, if nothin' else."

With those words, Dean realized that Skinner was no mere thug. The threats he had made before their voyage had done more than keep Dean in line. They had revealed the lengths Dean would go to in order to keep his friends safe. There was a twisted brilliance to Skinner's actions—impressive and reprehensible all at once.

"Guests," Dean said. "Is that how you see it?"

"That's all it has ta be. Same as before, how well everyone gets treated is up ta you. Do the job and I'll let you all go. Do it well, I might even give ya a share of the loot!"

Skinner turned his head and mugged for his crew, expecting them to balk at his offer. When they did, he made a playful show of reconsidering his generosity. "All right, half a share. Maybe. If I'm in a good mood when all's said and done. What'll it be, boy? Do we have a deal or not?"

Dean's mind was racing. He didn't trust Skinner to keep his word and let them go, and he didn't want to think what might become of his friends if he left them here alone.

"I told you, I don't do this kind of thing anymore. I'm out of practice."

"Bah! Yer a pirate, born and raised. It's in yer blood. I'm tired 'a' this conversation."

Marlon Spyke flashed his dagger and twirled it in his hand. "If I were you, I'd say yes while the captain's still askin' nicely."

"Maybe that's the problem," Long Tom Cannon said. "Could be we need to put it to him differently."

"Could be, Long Tom," Skinner agreed. "Let's see. Who's up for a swim?"

Long Tom grabbed Waverly. "How 'bout this one?" The big tree of a man picked her up as if she were a twig.

"Take your hands off her!" Verrick cried out. Marlon Spyke knocked the older man to the floor. Dean and Ronan started toward Waverly, but Long Tom threw her overboard before they got within two feet of her.

"Waverly!" Dean shouted. He reached the gunwales and prepared to dive in after her, but Skinner grabbed him by the collar and pulled him back.

"There's two ways we can do this. The hard way . . ." Skinner pointed to Waverly thrashing about in the ocean. "And the easy way." He held up a lifeline with a floater tied to the end. "I told you, I don't like hurtin' people 'less I have to. She doesn't have to drown out here. Say the word, and we'll reel 'er back in. It's not too late fer the lot of us ta be mates. Be smart about it, why don't ya?"

Dean stood still. His heart was in his throat as he watched Waverly treading water. He wanted to agree to whatever it took to get her back on deck before she was lost to the current. But Skinner was right—he had to be smart. He had to be every inch as ruthless and clever as his enemy if he wanted to survive. "Leave her." Dean pushed the line of rope away. "She's better off down there."

"What?" Verrick said.

"What?" Ronan echoed.

"*What?*" Waverly exclaimed. "Dean!"

Skinner studied Dean with a smirk. "Don't bluff me, boy. You don't mean that for a second. I can read you like a book."

"Read my *lips*," Dean said. "I'd rather see her drowned than up here with your ship full of rats."

Dean stood his ground as Skinner's eyes widened. Waverly's went even wider. "Dean, you scoundrel! Get me up there!"

Verrick struggled to his feet and sidled up to Dean. "What are you doing? Have you lost your mind?"

Dean said nothing. He was taking a huge risk, but it was all he could think to do. They weren't going to get anywhere if they kept playing by Skinner's rules. Dean had to change the game. He waited for everyone to get over their shock. It took forever.

"Blow me down, yer a stubborn one." Skinner shook his head. "Long Tom! Spyke! Grab the others and bind their hands and feet. We'll see if watchin' his friends sink ta the bottom don't soften his resolve."

Long Tom and Spyke went for Ronan and Verrick. Dean didn't budge an inch. "Throw them in too, see if I care," he called out. "Just know that any chance you have of getting that treasure goes with them." Skinner put up a hand and his men stood fast. "I need them with me, Skinner. When I went to Zenhala, I wasn't alone. These three were all there too. I need their help."

"Help?!" Waverly was aghast. "I'm not going to help you steal anything!"

Skinner cackled. "Don't worry lassie, no one's askin' ya to. I see yer game now, Seaborne. What do take me for, a fool?"

Dean shook his head. "I only wish. You're a bit too smart for my liking, but even you can't plan for everything. We don't know what we're going to find inside that castle. I've got a better chance of getting what you want if I've got my friends with me."

"A better chance of getting what *you* want, maybe. A better chance 'a' gettin' away." Skinner shook his head. "Sorry, yer friends stay here. Long Tom and Spyke can go with ya."

Dean snorted out a laugh. "Is that supposed to be a joke? You can clean those two up as much as you like, it won't matter. They're pirates to the bone. Everyone who claps eyes on them will know it. You know it too, or I wouldn't be here. I can do this, but I can't do it by myself."

Dean could tell his message had gotten through, but he also knew the wily captain wouldn't roll over that easy.

"I'm not giving up my hostages," Skinner said. "One of ya has to stay here. That's all there is to it."

"I'll stay," Verrick said instantly. "I'll do whatever you ask, just haul her up. Now!"

Skinner raised his eyebrows toward Dean and silently offered the rope once more. Dean nodded, and Skinner threw out the line.

As Long Tom Cannon reeled Waverly back in, Verrick whispered to Dean, "Don't worry about me. Just get her out of here and don't look back."

Dean said nothing. Verrick would have done anything to help free Waverly from Skinner's clutches. Dean had to find a way to do the same for Verrick. So far, all he had done was buy himself time to figure out his next move.

"It's settled then?" Skinner said. "We have a deal?"

Dean shook his head again. "Not yet."

"What now?"

"You need to understand this kind of thing doesn't happen overnight."

Skinner snickered at Dean's nerve. "Yer right about that. You've got until sundown to get us into that palace. Any longer than that, and yer man here's a goner."

"I need at least a week."

Skinner sniffed. "We all need things."

"Three days, then. Give me that long, at least. You misspoke before, Skinner. There's three ways to do this." Dean ticked them off on his fingers, one by one. "The easy way, the hard way, and the right way. If the job goes south, it's your neck on the line too. Don't you think it's worth the wait?"

"Two days," Skinner agreed at last. "And not an hour more."

Dean shook Skinner's hand. "Deal."

He went to help Waverly up onto the ship, but she slapped his hand away. "Don't touch me."

Skinner laughed as Verrick draped a blanket over Waverly's shoulders. "Women! There's just no pleasing 'em, is there?"

Dean glared at Skinner. "Let's not waste each other's time. Do you have a plan to get us in, or do I have to do everything?"

"Aye, lad. I like the way your mind works. Let's get down ta business."

CHAPTER 7

THE PLAN

"No one gets within a league of Aquatica if they don't look like they belong. You three might not pass for royalty . . ." Skinner paused to flap open a flag. "But I'll lay odds they let you in the servant's entrance, easy."

Dean took the flag and held it out for a look. Its symbol was a large black *A* set against a light blue field. Three wavy lines made up the *A*'s crossbar. "What is this?"

"It's yer ticket in, is what it is. We got it off a trio of circus performers bound fer Aquatica. That's how we found this place. Was them that had the heading."

Ronan frowned at the flag. "Circus performers? I don't understand."

"They was hired to entertain the guests." Marlon Spyke spun his dagger as he spoke. "Or, should I say, *you* three were hired. Savvy?"

Dean locked eyes with Spyke, then turned back to Skinner. He wasn't impressed with the plan. "What makes you think this will work?"

"*It'll work*," Skinner said. "Aquatica's chief talent scout, a man called Galen Fishback, caught their act in London and booked 'em ta play at the palace."

"Won't he cry foul when he sees we're not the people he hired?"

"We're pretty sure he won't even be there."

Dean blinked. "Pretty sure?"

"He'll be off to the next city, looking for the next great performer," Skinner said. "The way I hear it, people in that castle never know who he'll send their way next. They count on that flag as proof ya crossed paths with Fishback."

"How do you know all this?" Ronan asked.

Skinner's chest puffed up with pride. "The entertainers we raided spilled all. At first, they didn't want to give up nothin', but we got ways of askin' questions when we aren't tryin' ta be nice."

"Where are those men now?" Dean asked.

Skinner shrugged. "Like I said, we weren't tryin' ta be nice with them."

Waverly gasped. "You killed them?"

"You make it sound so unsavory. I told ya, it's just business. I couldn't have them catchin' on with some other ship and gettin' there ahead of us ta warn everybody. This here's the kind of job I can retire on. A resort full of nobles on holiday! Think about how those blue bloods pamper themselves at home. They *live* on vacation, that lot. I can only imagine what it must take ta spoil them out here."

"You're horrible," Waverly said.

"I can be, when things don't go my way. Somethin' you oughta know about me, lassie. Skinner ain't my Christian name. I earned that handle by deed. Just think on that whilst I got yer friend here keepin' me company these next few days."

"You don't have to keep threatening us," Dean said. "We've already agreed to take the job."

Skinner winked at Dean. "Just makin' sure." He nodded toward his ship. *Time to go.* Long Tom Cannon and Spyke took hold of Verrick. Dean watched helplessly as they marched him onto the deck of the *Crimson Tide*.

"We can't let them take Verrick," Waverly told Dean.

Dean shook his head. "We don't have a choice."

"Yes, we do! I won't let this happen!"

"It's all right Waverly," Verrick called back. "This is what I'm here for."

"No, it's not! I forbid you to go with them!"

"She forbids it!" Long Tom Cannon exclaimed. "What kind of men let a girl talk to them like this?"

Waverly flushed with anger and stormed up to the gunwales.

For a moment, Dean was afraid she might give herself away as a Zenhalan princess. She may not have cared for her royal title, but she didn't care to be condescended to either. From the deck of Skinner's ship, Verrick shook his head. The look on his face was urgent, his message crystal clear: *Don't put yourself at risk. Let me do this for you, please!*

"Are we going to have a problem here?" Skinner asked.

"No," Dean said. "There's no problem. *Is there*, Waverly?"

Waverly held her tongue but still threw Dean a look to make the devil run and hide.

"That's more like it," Skinner said as he took his leave of the *Tideturner*. "It's a simple job, this is. Go in pretendin' ta be the troupe 'a' performers what we raided. Fly that flag and tell 'em who hired ya. Galen Fishback. Remember that name. You got two days, Seaborne. I'll look to the east every morning at dawn. Signal me with a looking glass when yer ready. When I signal back, you'll know I'm coming. I want to be greeted by open gates, you hear? Open gates!"

Skinner's crew gave the railing of the *Tideturner* a heavy shove with their boots. That was that. They were off.

CHAPTER 8

ONCE A SPY

Dean and his friends sailed in silence until Skinner's ship was out of earshot. They went on that way a good while afterward as well.

Dean felt lower than the ocean floor. Forced back into the service of pirates. He had thought himself done with that life, but apparently *it* wasn't yet done with him.

"Chin up, Seaborne. It's not all bad," Ronan said. "For one thing, you're not in jail anymore. For another, this job at least squares with the Gentleman's Code."

Dean's eyes remained fixed on the deck of the ship.

"What code?" Waverly asked.

"My old captain's code," Ronan explained. "Gentleman Jim

Harper. He was a good man, nothing like Skinner and his crew. Captain Harper made sure we only stole from people who could afford it, people who deserved it, or both."

"And where is this gentleman now?" Waverly said *gentleman* with enough sarcasm to melt a cannonball.

"Lost at sea," Ronan said mournfully. "But not before he saved me and Seaborne's life. I couldn't do the same for him, but I can honor his memory. If anyone can afford to get robbed, Aquatica's royal guests can."

Dean shook his head. "We said the same thing on our way to Zenhala, remember? Legends are tricky, Ronan. We don't know what we're going to find once we reach Aquatica."

Ronan grimaced. "What are we going to do if the legends aren't true this time?"

"Devil if I know," Dean said.

"It doesn't matter if the legends are true or not," Waverly said. "We have to warn the people in that castle about Skinner. We have to ask them for help. *That's* what we're going to do."

"It's not that simple," Dean said.

"Why not?"

"Because they don't know us," Ronan explained. "They don't have any reason to trust or help us."

"That doesn't mean they won't."

"We can't take that chance," Dean said.

"Suddenly you're so cautious?" Waverly said. "You seemed

perfectly happy to risk our lives back there with Skinner."

"That was different," Dean said. "It was in his best interest to meet me halfway. You're talking about relying on the kindness of strangers. That's a bad bet."

Waverly scoffed. "If all you ever do is lie to everyone you meet, you don't give them much chance to show you any kindness, do you? I understand you don't have much experience with the truth, but you might be surprised where it gets you."

"I'll be surprised if it doesn't get us killed," Dean said. "Best-case scenario, they'll throw us in the brig and blast Skinner's ship to matchwood. That's what I'd do."

"That's what you'd do?" Waverly was appalled. "Verrick is on board that ship."

"That's what I'd do if I were *them*. He's nothing to them."

Waverly looked away.

"I didn't say he was nothing to *me*," Dean said. "You're not really mad I told Skinner to leave you in the ocean, are you? I was bluffing! I had to do something to get us off that ship."

"I'm off that ship because Verrick volunteered to take my place. We are *not* leaving him to die. Just so we're clear."

"Who said anything about leaving him to die? I never said that!"

"And we're not helping Skinner raid that castle either," Waverly said. "Gentleman's Code or not, mountains of treasure or not . . . it doesn't matter. Maybe you weren't paying attention at your trial, but I was. People die in pirate raids, and if the stories about Aquatica are true, the most valuable thing behind its walls will be the guests. Skinner will take as many royal hostages as he can and put the rest to the sword. I don't want any part of that."

"You think I do?" Dean asked.

"I think you couldn't leave your pirate life behind even if you wanted to."

"What do you mean *if* I wanted to?"

Waverly didn't answer. An icy quiet filled the air between her and Dean. They were standing only three feet apart, but she might as well have been miles away.

"We're nearly there," Ronan said, breaking the silence. "The wind is with us, if nothing else." The fortress grew larger with each passing wave. "The castle blends in because of its color. An easy enough thing to miss at a distance, but up close . . ."

Dean, Ronan, and Waverly marveled at the sight of Aquatica—massive, foreboding—as the *Tideturner* closed in.

A crescent-shaped bed of volcanic rock made up the foundation of the fortress-at-sea. The castle boasted a circular base and walls of blue-gray stone that angled up to form an open-air dome. Three towers grew out of the exterior, supported by iron beams rooted in the fortress's stone footing. Each tower rose to a different height, but they all had the same sparkling headpiece: huge plates of sea glass, curled together like flower buds.

Shiny brass cannons topped the ramparts, but Dean saw no gunners manning the weapons. Though Aquatica was big enough to hold a thousand people, the place was silent as a church. And from the looks of things, unguarded.

"It's quiet," Waverly said. "Why's it so quiet? And what are those?"

A network of large metal spheres surrounded the castle, floating in the water. Sturdy chains appeared to hold the spheres in place. "Mines," Dean said. "We touch one of those and we're done for. Ronan, you'll have to take her straight in."

"Aye," Ronan said. The water leading up to the main gate appeared to be free of the mines. "I'll steer clear, but a well-aimed cannonball will sink us just as easy. You'd better run up that—"

The boom of cannon fire interrupted Ronan, and a geyser of flame erupted from the ocean. Waverly screamed, "What was that?"

Dean spun around to look at the mast. There was nothing hanging off it but the sails. "The flag!" He ran to hoist their colors. He had been so busy arguing with Waverly that he had forgotten to run up the flag!

"Did we hit a mine?" Waverly asked, looking over the side of the ship.

"No, they did," Ronan called back. "Triggered the blast with a cannonball. It was a warning shot."

"Some warning!"

"Still think honesty is the best policy?" Dean asked. Working as fast as he could, he tied the flag to the line and pulled down, hand over hand, to send it up. The whole time, he was certain the next cannonball—the one to sink them—would be coming over any second. Two more shots were fired, and two more fiery explosions shook the water around their ship.

He raised the flag Skinner gave them and turned around to look at the castle. A large circular gate dominated the fortress's main wall. Dean held his breath as the *Tideturner* closed in on the front door.

But the cannons remained silent. The next sound Dean heard came from a faint voice all the way up at the top of the wall. "Sorry about that!" the voice called down. "Welcome, travelers! Do come in!"

CHAPTER 9

Aquatica

Dean exhaled in relief and slumped against the mast. After a heavy click-clack behind the fortress gate, a portion of the massive round door slid up, creating an opening the shape of a slice of pie, large enough to admit the *Tideturner*.

The three friends looked at each other as Ronan took the ship in. No one spoke, but it was plain to see they were all thinking the same thing.

That was too close.

As they entered the castle, another thought took over:

Where is everyone?

The castle was bare on the inside. Once through the gate, Dean discovered that the imposing fortress walls were merely barriers built up around a lagoon. Wooden decking sat upon the rocky foundation and made up the castle floor. It ran around the interior walls, leaving a vast pool of open water in the center. Ronan brought the ship in close and dropped anchor. Dean jumped out to tie the ship off at a piling. His stomach tightened as he took in the vacant space before him. Heavy chains hung down from an iron ring that sat atop the open roof. Outside, the castle had looked extravagant and beautiful. Inside, it was as cold, functional, and silent as the grave.

"What now?" Ronan asked. "Even if we did sneak Skinner in here, there's nothing for him to steal."

"This is what I was afraid of," Dean said. "Legends only tell you half the story."

"Maybe he can tell us the other half." Waverly pointed at a lone figure on the ramparts across the water. The man started down a flight of stairs built into the wall.

"I'm sure he can," Dean said. "Let's just be careful what we tell him in return."

The stranger hastened to join them. He was a stout gentleman with a shiny bald head, bags under his eyes, and round chubby cheeks. Maybe it was a trick of the light, but Dean thought the man's coloring seemed a bit off. He didn't look well.

"Sorry! Sorry! Sorry about the shooting," the man said upon reaching the group. "Is everyone all right?" he asked, huffing and wheezing. "Please tell me no one's been injured!" The man spoke with an accent Dean had never heard before.

"We're alive," Ronan said. "Even if you did scare us half to death."

"I didn't know who you were! You can't blame a man for being careful, can you? You might have been pirates. How should I know?"

"Pirates!" Dean gave a nervous laugh. "What an idea."

"You're supposed to fly the flag on approach," the man said. "Did he not tell you that?"

"He?" Dean probed.

"Sir Fishback! Who else? You are the entertainers he hired, aren't you?"

"That's right. Galen Fishback," Dean confirmed. "He hired us to perform, but—"

"Where have you been? It's been weeks since I saw him. Everyone's waiting!"

Waverly looked around at the empty castle. "Everyone?"

"Not here," the man said. "There's no one *here*. Well, not unless you count me. I suppose I should introduce myself, shouldn't I? That would help. I am Mookergwog, Keeper of Aquatica. Welcome, my friends, welcome! I'm so glad I didn't blow you up." He breathed heavily, giving them all a hearty shake and then fanning himself.

"Are you all right?" Waverly asked.

"I'm fine. I don't usually run all the way down these steps. I like to take my time."

"Of course, but I don't mean that. It's . . ." Waverly paused. She was trying to be delicate. "Are you sure you're not sick?"

Mookergwog tapped his chest. "Fit as a fiddle. Why do you ask?"

Waverly, Ronan, and Dean looked at each other. Up close, there was no denying it. Mookergwog's skin was green. Perhaps not a deep green like seaweed, but at least a pale jade. The man himself seemed oblivious to it.

"I'm confused," Ronan said, changing the subject. "If the castle is empty, why were you shooting at us? And who in blazes are we here to entertain?"

"I think we're all a little confused," Dean agreed. "We were told this place was a holiday retreat for noble patrons."

"I'm afraid we haven't been entirely honest with you," Mookergwog confessed.

Dean touched a hand to his chest, feigning shock. "We've been lied to?"

"You'll forgive me once I tell you why," Mookergwog said. "You might even be excited! Most men are. If I had my druthers, I'd be going with you."

"Going with us?" Dean said. "We've only just arrived."

Mookergwog shook his head. "This is not your true destination. You were hired to entertain royalty, and that you will surely do. But not here."

"What are you talking about?" Ronan asked. "Where are we going?"

"Aquatica isn't what you've been led to believe, friends. It's merely a border station."

"A border station?" Dean said.

"What exactly are we on the border of?" Waverly asked.

Mookergwog smiled and waved a hand at the water. "The greatest kingdom in all the sea. Atlantis."

CHAPTER 10

AN UNEXPECTED JOURNEY

"Atlantis?" Dean blurted.

Ronan backed away from Mookergwog as if the man had a disease. "You're mad."

Mookergwog laughed. "They all say that. But answer me this." He raised a finger in the air. "If I'm such a nutter, where'd I get this lovely green suntan? That's right, I saw you staring," he added, looking at Waverly. "Or do you suppose my madness is contagious and the lot of you are seeing things?"

Dean opened his mouth but didn't speak. Mookergwog had a point.

"It's always this way. Sir Fishback's talent scouts scour the globe, searching for the most amazing people the surface world has to offer. We invite world-class performers like yourselves to come take the stage at 'Aquatica,' but we must wait until the final moment to reveal the truth. It's safer that way. No one shows up at my door believing in Atlantis, much less expecting to go there. I'm used to dealing with doubters."

Atlantis! Dean thought. *Could it be?*

Instead of simply assuming that Mookergwog was trying to trick him, as per his natural instinct, he took a moment to rethink the situation from a different angle. An Atlantean angle, perhaps. The intense secrecy around the castle, coupled with its barren interior, made more sense from that perspective. So did the castle's advanced defenses and the explosive welcome he and his mates had received—to say nothing of Mookergwog's green skin.

Unbelievable as it was, it wasn't so hard to believe.

"We can't go to Atlantis!" Waverly said.

Mookergwog snickered and rubbed his hands together. "There's always one. In every group that turns up here, there's always one worrywart. No disrespect intended.

"Lots of people get cold feet at this point in the journey," Mookergwog continued. "It's perfectly natural. Not to worry, little lady, there's air to breathe down there. Plenty of it. You have my word."

Waverly crossed her arms. "Little lady?"

"We should introduce ourselves," Dean said, trying to help Mookergwog extricate his foot from his mouth. "Her name is

Waverly, I'm Dean, and this is Ronan."

"My honored guests," Mookergwog said, bowing. "Again, welcome. Your presence breathes life into this empty castle."

"Speaking of breathing and life," Ronan began, "you say there's air to breathe down there? How's that possible?"

"It's not! But it is! It's extraordinary. Wait until you see it, lad. It'll steal your breath away. Not literally, of course. Figure of speech . . ." He paused and cleared his throat. "Look. I understand you might have reservations. Some things in life have to be seen in order to be believed. For now, just trust that everything I'm telling you is true. There's nothing to be afraid of."

"I'm not afraid," Waverly said. "The reason we can't go is because—"

Don't do it, Dean told her with his eyes. *Don't tell him about Skinner . . .*

Mookergwog interrupted Waverly first: "Come now, this is Atlantis we're talking about! A once-in-a-lifetime opportunity! Not only is it capital of the Mer-World, it's home to three of the Seven Great Wonders of the Sea. The Magic Mountains. The Water Tower. The Blood of Poseidon!"

Dean, Ronan, and Waverly had no idea what Mookergwog was talking about, and he didn't bother to explain.

"Without question, it's the greatest city ever built beneath the waves," Mookergwog continued. "Nothing in the Clearwater Kingdoms or the Trenchlands even comes close."

"You mean to say there's more than one underwater city?" Ronan asked.

"There's more than one city up on land, isn't there? What makes you think it's any different down below? But, mark me well, Atlantis is the best of them. Atlantis is special. I'm jealous of you three. If I had my druthers, I'd be going with you. And to think you're getting paid to make the trip. Handsomely, I might add!"

"Paid?" Dean's ears perked up. "I'm sorry, say that last part again?"

Mookergwog scoffed. "Did Fishback tell you nothing? Of course you're getting paid. Queen Avenel is most generous. Win her favor and she'll reward you with gold, rubies, pearls . . . whatever you fancy."

"Truly?" Dean said.

"On my honor," Mookergwog said, placing a hand over his heart. "If the audience loves you, so will she. The more heads you turn, the more coins you'll count, if you get my meaning."

"I do," Dean said, mulling over the possibilities. "Mookergwog, could my mates and I perhaps have a moment to discuss this privately?"

"Take all the time you need," Mookergwog replied. "And take this as well." He produced a large leather-bound book and handed it to Ronan.

"What's this?" Ronan asked.

"The Customs Ledger for Atlantis. Everyone who visits the

city has to sign in and out. You three can add your names . . . once you realize you'd be mad not to go." He threw the group a wink and backed away, granting them room to talk things over.

"I can't believe I'm saying this, but I think he might be right," Dean told his friends. "We might have found the solution to our problem."

"What solution?" asked Waverly. "We can't leave this place. We have to stay and help Verrick."

"We have to *go* so we can help Verrick," Dean contended.

"Seaborne's right," Ronan agreed. "If this is real, it's the answer to our prayers. Especially yours, Waverly. We wouldn't even have to steal anything. We can use what they pay us to buy Verrick's life." He tapped Dean's shoulder. "What are 'druthers,' by the way?"

"I don't know, but it sounds like if you have them, you can do anything. Maybe we should ask for them as part of our payment."

Waverly sighed. "No one's going to pay us anything. Not unless there's some play you two have been rehearsing in secret. Tell me, Ronan, what's your performance going to be about?"

Ronan shrugged. "I didn't say I've worked out all the details."

"You haven't worked out any. Even if Atlantis is real and we manage to pull this off, what makes you think Skinner will be satisfied with our offer? You say we can pay him enough gold to buy our freedom. When it comes to gold, I doubt there's a pirate living who knows the meaning of the word *enough*."

"You're looking at two of them right now," Dean said.

"I nearly forgot, you trained at the feet of an *honorable* pirate. I heard all about it in court."

"Hold on," Ronan said. "You can run down Seaborne all you like, but don't you besmirch the good name of Gentleman Jim Harper."

Dean looked to Waverly. "What would you have us do?"

"Tell Mookergwog the truth. With his help, we can ambush Skinner and free Verrick."

"How? Even if he agrees to help us, we're still hopelessly outnumbered. Are you trying to get Verrick killed?"

"Are *you*?" Waverly asked. "We don't even know how far away Atlantis is. It could be a week's journey from here. Skinner gave us two days."

"Mookergwog! How long does it take to reach Atlantis?" Ronan called out, leafing through the Customs Ledger.

"Five minutes at most," their green-skinned host called back.

"Five minutes!" Dean and Waverly both said. Mookergwog's answer wasn't just surprising, it was impossible.

"That settles it," Ronan said. "We're going."

Waverly's mouth fell open. "What are you talking about? We haven't settled anything."

"We're going," Ronan said again. "Look here." He spun the ledger around so Dean and Waverly could read it. One entry stood out from all the others. Down at the bottom of the page, written in strong, artful letters, was the name *James Harper*.

CHAPTER 11

ATLANTIS HO!

"You see that? He signed in, but he never signed out. He must still be down there!"

Ronan was practically floating on air. Dean tried to pull him back down to earth. "I don't know, Ronan. I wouldn't get my hopes up too high."

Waverly was more direct. "You said he was dead."

"I said he was lost at sea," Ronan said. "Maybe he found his way here?"

"That doesn't sound very likely."

"Aye, Ronan." Dean put a hand on his friend's shoulder. "I hate to say it, but I'm not sure which idea I find harder to believe. Atlantis being real or Gentleman Jim being down there waiting for us."

"He's got to be there," Ronan said. "Look at the date he signed this. Just weeks after our ship went down." He waved at Mookergwog, beckoning him to rejoin the group.

"Mookergwog!" Ronan said, holding up the book. "What can you tell me about this man? Can you describe him at all?"

Mookergwog squinted at the signature. "Who's that, Harper? Let's see . . . yes, I remember. He was a tall man. Strong build, brown hair, a beard . . . His mates had a special name for him."

"What did they call him?" asked Dean.

Mookergwog rubbed his chin. "I couldn't tell you why, but everyone called him The Gentleman."

"Might that have been Gentleman *Jim*?" Ronan asked.

Mookergwog snapped his fingers. "That was it. Gentleman Jim. How did you—"

"I knew it!" Ronan smacked Dean on the shoulder. "He's alive. Alive!"

"Blow me down," Dean said. *What next?* "How did he end up here?"

"You'd have to ask him that," Mookergwog said. "He came through with a theater company, months ago. I only remember him because they let him stay down there, the lucky devil. You know him?"

Ronan nodded. "We know him."

"How's that for luck?" Mookergwog laughed. "Not only do you three get to visit Atlantis, but you've got a friend inside the city to boot." He nudged Waverly. "I reckon you feel better about making the trip now, eh, love?"

Waverly put on a fake smile. "You have no idea." She could tell it was no use arguing now. They were going to Atlantis whether she liked it or not.

"How do we get there?" Ronan asked. "How soon can we leave?"

"And what kind of a ship is going to get us there in five minutes?" Dean wanted to know.

Mookergwog wagged a finger. "It's not the ship that does it. It's the Waterways. I told you, Atlantis is special. A place where all the wonders in the deep blue sea come together. You surface-dwellers don't know it, but there are secret currents down below that lead all around the world. The Waterways are like enchanted rivers, flowing under the sea, and this castle's right on top of one." Mookergwog pulled the tarp off a large iron sphere with a hatch built into the side. "Your chariot awaits."

Dean peered through the heavy glass pane covering the porthole hatch. Inside, he saw four tiny seats covered with velvet and secured with thick leather belts. He tapped on the pod's metal hull. "You're sure this thing won't leak?"

"Not a chance. I built that ship myself and triple-checked every bolt. She'll hold together."

"It looks like a giant mine," Waverly said.

"No." Mookergwog shook his head, smiling. "I designed those to come apart dramatically. This ship? Tight as a drum."

"I'm satisfied," Ronan said.

"I'm not." Waverly backed away. "I'm not getting in there. No way."

"I wouldn't send you down there to drown," Mookergwog said. "Honestly, there's nothing to be afraid of."

"I'm not afraid," Waverly said. "I just don't like tight spaces."

"It'll be over before you know it," Mookergwog assured her. "The ride alone is worth the trip, and once you reach the city? Your eyes will pop out of your head!" He caught himself. "That's another figure of speech, you understand . . . I'm not doing a good job of explaining things, am I?"

"You're doing fine," Ronan said, patting Mookergwog on the back. "Don't be difficult, Waverly. I followed you to St. Blanc."

"You complained every step of the way, if I recall."

"We still went, didn't we? It's time to even up the scales. Come on, Seaborne, let's get this ship in the water."

Dean looked at Waverly as if his hands were tied and went to help Ronan rock the pod off its base. Together, they rolled it to the edge of the platform, where Mookergwog hooked it with the chains that hung down from the ring overhead. Once he had steadied the ship, Ronan wasted no time getting in.

"We're leaving already?" Waverly asked.

"No time like the present," Ronan called back.

"No time to waste, either," Dean added.

Mookergwog offered a hand to help Waverly get on board.

"Come on, lass, it'll be an adventure. You might even enjoy it."

Dean could tell Waverly wasn't pleased with the impression Mookergwog had of her. She didn't like being thought of as some jittery jitterbug. "I don't have a problem with adventure," she said. "I told you, I just don't like—"

"Tight spaces, I know. Just close your eyes and pretend you're sailing 'cross the sea instead of under it. Before you can count to ten, you'll have a whole city to stretch out in."

Waverly reluctantly climbed on top of the pod and went in feet first.

Dean entered the pod last. Ronan had settled in the back row, strapped in and ready to go. Waverly was in one of the front seats, struggling with a belt and looking very uncomfortable. Dean sat down next to her and assessed the panel in front of him. Save for a single wooden handle, the ship had no controls. "How does this work?"

Mookergwog stuck his head in the window. "Nothing to it. First, buckle up. All of you. Those belts will keep you in your seats no matter which way the tides take you. I'm going to go outside and chain an anchor to the ship to pull you under. Once you've submerged and hit the current, pull that lever to drop the weight, and away you go."

"How will I know when we hit the current?" Dean asked.

Mookergwog grinned. "Don't worry. You'll know."

"Why don't you come with us? There's room for one more." Dean thought, if nothing else, Waverly might feel more comfortable with Mookergwog at the controls. The green man shook his head sadly.

"I wish I could, lad, but I've got a job to do up here. Now, Godspeed." He rapped his knuckles on the outside of the ship. "Enjoy the ride. I expect to hear all about your trip upon your return."

With that, Mookergwog closed the hatch and sealed them in. Darkness filled most of the pod. The porthole admitted only a narrow beam of light. Dean looked over at Waverly. She was holding her breath. It didn't matter how much of a thrill-seeker she was in every other aspect of her life. Whenever Waverly got stuck in some place too restricting, she became a different person—paralyzed by fear. She could even be a danger to herself and others. Dean had seen it happen. He tried to reassure her, but the slightest touch made her skin crawl.

"Don't. Just . . . don't."

He realized she must have been feeling like this the whole time Skinner had them locked up. Confined to quarters on the ship for days, and they'd only been out a couple hours. Now here she was, boxed in again.

"Waverly, I know you don't want to be here, but trust me, this is the right thing to do."

"Because you're all about doing the right thing, aren't you, Dean?"

Dean sat up in his seat. "What's that supposed to mean?"

"You're risking Verrick's life for a *pirate*," Waverly said.

"Hey!" Ronan said from the backseat. "We used to be pirates too, don't forget."

"And we're not going down there to help Skinner sack the city or steal a single gold coin," Dean added. "This is the best shot we have at saving Verrick without anyone getting hurt. And I realize you don't know Gentleman Jim, but if there's even a tiny chance that he's down there, we have to take that chance. This is the right choice. It's the only choice."

"It is now that we've backed ourselves into a corner," Waverly said, her voice bitter. "I blame myself for that."

"What are you talking about?"

"I should never have gone to sea with you in the first place."

Dean felt as if Waverly had just punched him in the gut. "What?"

"This is wrong. Everything about it. When we left Zenhala together, I thought I knew who you were and what to expect. It was supposed to be fun and adventure. Now we're at the mercy of Skinner and his pirate crew, you've fallen right back into life as a spy, and we're hopping from one lie to the next. Verrick's got two days to live, but your main concern is saving your old pirate captain."

"That's not fair," Dean said.

"Don't talk to me about fair. None of this is fair," Waverly replied. "This isn't my life. I don't belong here."

Dean was lost for words. It wasn't supposed to be his life either. Not anymore.

Ronan leaned in over Dean's shoulder. "I told you this wouldn't end well."

"Shut up, Ronan."

An uncomfortable silence fell over the pod, broken only by the loud clink-clank of chains being dragged along the dock. They couldn't see Mookergwog anymore, but they could hear him working to latch something onto the front of the pod. He gave the hull of the ship a tap and called out, "Bon voyage!"

With a heavy metal scraping sound followed by a splash, the pod lurched into the water. Waverly yelped as they flipped around to face the ocean floor. Strapped securely into their plush velvet seats, she, Dean, and Ronan hung there suspended as the anchor pulled them down. They were sinking fast.

A phosphorescent strip of water came into view down below the ship. Just a glowing line at first, it grew larger with each passing second. After the first minute of the pod's steady descent, the water's cool, blue light entered its cabin. Dean leaned forward, getting as close to the window as his belt would allow.

"Look at that," he said, marveling at the luminous path ahead. It had an eerie, supernatural quality, like the tail of a sea serpent or the wake of a ghost ship.

Waverly was breathing in short staccato bursts. "Let go of the anchor."

"We're not there yet. If I drop it now, we'll float right back up."

Waverly made a face that said, *fine by me.*

"You're going to miss it," Ronan told Dean.

"I'm not going to miss it."

"Hard to starboard, now!" Ronan shouted.

"Is it your understanding that I'm somehow steering this ship? We're sinking, Ronan. That's all."

Dean waited until the bright streak of water was upon them. As soon as they hit the Waterway, an incredible force took hold of the vessel. Dean detached the anchor and the current carried them off. They weren't sinking anymore. They were flying—under the sea.

PART THREE

DEEP COVER

CHAPTER 12

Getting There Is Half the Fun

The Waterway sucked Dean, Ronan, and Waverly deep into the ocean at a speed that Dean would never have thought possible. The acceleration was amazing. In mere seconds, they had gone from a standstill to traveling faster than the wind. Faster than Dean had ever gone before, even on his kiteboard.

Deeper and deeper, faster and faster, the ship swirled around as it advanced. The topsy-turvy craft flipped them every which way until the words *up* and *down* lost all meaning. Dean took deep breaths, trying to pull himself together despite the endless rotations. The constant spinning made him feel sick. He wasn't alone.

"I feel sick," groaned Ronan.

"Don't you throw up in here, Ronan. Don't you dare!"

Ronan leaned his head back and closed his eyes. He looked greener than Mookergwog. Dean and Waverly traded looks that were equal parts revulsion and fear. The thought of Ronan losing his lunch on the way to Atlantis was too horrible to imagine. Dean would have rather seen the ship spring a leak.

Thankfully, the pod stabilized a minute later, locking into place within the current, oriented right-side up. Dean breathed a sigh of relief when everything stopped spinning. A fresh headache replaced that sensation. Having found its groove in the water, the pod surged forward like a ship being boosted by a strong tailwind. Soon they were going so fast Dean couldn't move. He struggled to breathe normally, feeling his face flatten as invisible forces pushed him back into his chair. From the corner of his eye, he saw Waverly's cheeks trying hard to touch her ears.

The pressure was intense as they raced with the current, following the greedy pull of the Waterway. The pod took turns hard and fast, spinning them around to face backward, sideways, and every odd angle in between. Everyone let out yelps and whoops as the snakelike underwater channel took unexpected dips and rounded unseen corners.

Dean began to wonder how far they had traveled. How many fathoms? How many leagues? He wished he could see where they were going. He had a limited view through the porthole, but it was a once-in-a-lifetime view just the same.

They hurtled past sharks, whales, and all manner of sea life. The water changed color, growing darker as they moved deeper into the ocean. As the light faded, glowing crystals on the interior walls of the pod lit up. Until that moment, Dean had assumed they were purely decorative. He had only noted them as something to possibly steal. Old habits. Like it or not, his life as a pirate spy was all coming back to him. Dean tried to reach out and touch one of the glimmering gemstones, but the ship was still moving too fast for him to lift his arm.

A layer of frost appeared on the porthole window. Dean shivered and saw his breath freeze in front of his face. The vapors, rising like smoke in the air, shocked him. *Does it get that cold down here?* he wondered. *What's it going to be like at the bottom? We're going to freeze to death!*

But the depth of the water was not to blame for the drop in temperature. The Waterway current led the pod climbing back up toward the surface, and Dean spotted icebergs above them. They were skirting the coast of the South Pole—the very bottom of the earth! Or maybe it was the North Pole. Dean couldn't tell. He couldn't believe it. Could they really have gone so far, so fast?

Warm water soon banished the arctic chill, as the pod rocketed back toward the equator at impossible speeds. Things got tropical again as they approached their final destination. They had to be nearly there. Mookergwog had said the whole journey would only take five minutes.

The pod took an abrupt drop straight down, and Dean's stomach jumped up into his throat. It was as if they had fallen into a deep, dark pit. The soft, crystalline glow returned to light up the interior of the pod as they fell. Through the window, Dean saw another far-off light outside the pod. It started out like a distant star but grew larger and more brilliant the closer they got, until Dean had to shut his eyes. The pod swooped down and up like it was exiting a ramp. Everyone was thrown forward as the pod came out of the Waterway with a jolt.

Able to move once more, Dean stretched out his arms, rubbing his eyes to shield them from the blinding light outside the window. A gentle current carried them forward, and the pod turned away from the intense white glare. As Dean's eyes adjusted, he saw where the light was coming from. Whole mountain ranges of luminescent crystals, just like the ones inside the pod, lit up the sandy bottom of the sea. The ship weaved slowly around their jagged peaks and sharp edges until Dean saw it. Atlantis. The legendary underwater kingdom was right in front of them.

The city sat under a transparent dome of running water. Spouting from a central point above the city, it fell in continuous waves like a waterfall under the sea. Dean, Ronan, and Waverly were awestruck. Dean felt half-delirious from the trip.

"I'm not the only one seeing this, am I?"

Ronan leaned forward. "I see it, but I don't believe it."

Glowing rock formations spiraled out from the city's base, bathing the whole area with a radiant luster.

"These must be the Magic Mountains," Dean said. Smaller rocks and minerals littered the ocean floor all around them, sparkling like diamonds. He saw people swimming around in the water outside the city, both mermen and mermaids. Some of them swam on their own while others coursed through the water on the backs of giant sea horses. Mookergwog had spoken the truth. The Atlantean seascape was breathtaking. The full sprawl extended past the edge of the city to a bustling reef town with coral towers, but the bulk of Atlantis—and the most impressive structures within it—all stood under the dome. Dean could make out tall buildings, stately temples, and a castle that rivaled the Aqualine Palace of Zenhala.

A slow, twisting current carried the pod forward. Dean and his friends enjoyed the view and the new relaxed pace until they drew even with the ocean floor. Dean put them at half a league away from the city. The path ahead was bounded on either side by statues carved from the same incandescent minerals that were strewn about everywhere else. Sculptures of what must have been Atlantean warriors lined the path.

The guiding current brought the pod toward the aqua-dome that surrounded Atlantis, but at the last second, something shadowy and strong pulled Dean and his friends off course. Whatever it was carried them around to the other side of the city and swung the pod through the watery barrier there. The vessel hit dry sand and rolled on like a cannonball tumbling across the deck of a ship. When at last the pod came to a stop, Dean unbuckled himself and opened the door. He stood up, poking his head out through the hatch. Dizzy and overstimulated, he made a conscious effort to not fall over.

When Dean finally steadied himself, the first thing he noticed was the welcome committee. A platoon of soldiers in heavy black armor had them surrounded, weapons out. *Nice to meet you too,* Dean thought.

Ronan was the first one to greet them in turn, clawing past Dean and throwing up all over the outside of the pod. Dean patted Ronan's back as he wretched.

"Way to hold it together, Ronan. Good job."

CHAPTER 13

WELCOME TO ATLANTIS

"**D**on't move," one of the soldiers ordered. He was a big man, over six feet tall.

Dean replied with a wobbly nod of the head. *Works for me.* At the moment, his goal was to move as little as possible. The journey had turned his bones to jelly. Now that it had ended, he could barely stand up straight. Every time he turned his head, the world swung around violently. Dean closed his eyes and waited for the vertigo to pass. Ronan remained slumped over the outside of the pod, looking like he might get sick again.

Waverly squeezed her way through the door to get a look outside. The front line of soldiers rushed the pod when she emerged.

"What is this? What's going on?" Waverly's voice was just above a whisper.

Dean eyed the soldiers uncomfortably. "No idea."

This was not the greeting that any of them had expected to receive. The soldiers before them were nothing like Mookergwog, either in manner or appearance. They had charcoal gray skin, bright red eyes, and suits of armor that had been crafted from the shells of giant crabs and lobsters. They were armed with claw-shaped gauntlets and swords edged with jagged, uneven teeth. To a man, they all sported the same menacing look on their faces. It was highly unlikely that any of them could be reasoned with, but Dean tried his best.

"I think there's been some kind of misunderstanding. We were sent here to—"

"Save your breath," the large soldier said. "Our captain will decide what's to be done with you."

"Your captain? We were promised an audience with the queen."

The soldier said nothing. Dean could tell it was no use pushing the man further. All they could do was wait and hope the man in charge was friendlier than the men who served underneath him.

As Dean looked around for the missing captain, his eyes flashed up to the miraculous liquid dome flowing down around the city. He didn't understand how such a thing could hold back the ocean, but there was no denying that it did its job ably.

Dean's legs steadied beneath him, but the breadth and grandeur of Atlantis remained a dizzying sight. Everywhere he looked, he saw tall spires and grand temples supported by massive columns. He had never seen such a city, with so much packed into one place. Countless buildings filled every inch of space under the dome. Some of them climbed so high, Dean worried they might fall over. And it was colorful, a kaleidoscope of pastels. Everything was pristine and beautiful, carved from clean, smooth sandstone and a rainbow array of corals.

Taking in the unnatural nature of Atlantis, Dean had to pinch himself to make sure he wasn't dreaming. Dry sand on the ocean floor, packed down tight, the consistency of hard clay. And air—he was breathing air, thousands of feet beneath the waves. A bucket of cold water splashed onto Dean's sense of wonder as a fierce-looking woman pushed through the ring of soldiers. Apparently, the man in charge was a woman.

She was beautiful, with stormy gray skin and red eyes flecked with gold. She had long straight hair, so black that it shone, and thick, full lips. The woman paced along the ground before them like a predator sizing up her prey. A suit of light armor covered her athletic frame like a second skin. As she passed Dean, he spotted curved knives tucked into scabbards that had been built into the padding on her back.

"Commander, what's the meaning of this?" the woman demanded. "Who are these children?"

"Captain." The tall soldier straightened his back. "You ordered us to detain the next pod that arrived from the surface. These children are its passengers."

The captain frowned at Dean and the others. She took a step closer. "What are your intentions here? Who sent you?"

"We were hired by Galen Fishback," Dean said, his voice cracking as the words came out. "Is that all right?"

"Fishback." The captain put on a dour expression. "Very clever. Who would ever suspect these innocent faces?"

Dean squinted. "Suspect us? Of what? I'm afraid we're getting off on the wrong foot here. Let's back up. My name is Dean Seaborne. My companions are—"

"I don't need your names."

"We're entertainers hired to put on a show. Nothing more."

"You think I don't know when I'm being lied to? Commander!"

She barked out a series of orders in a language Dean didn't understand. The next thing Dean knew, the soldiers pulled him out of the pod and marched Dean and his friends up to the edge of the city.

"What are you doing?" Dean protested. "I don't understand!"

"What's going on?" Ronan asked, coming out of his funk.

Waverly struggled in a soldier's grasp. "Unhand me! We haven't done anything wrong!"

No one was listening. The soldiers held them inches away from the watery barrier that separated Atlantis from the ocean.

"I'm going to give you one chance to tell me your true purpose in Atlantis. You can either talk or you can swim home. The choice is yours."

"This is crazy!" Ronan shouted. "Why are you doing this?"

"I want the truth," the captain said. Her voice was cold and unforgiving. "Tell me the real reason you came to Atlantis. I won't ask again."

A soldier pushed Dean's nose into the rushing water. "All right!" Dean shouted. He was about to reveal everything from Skinner to Gentleman Jim when a new voice called out:

"Halt!"

Dean held his tongue. He heard footsteps approaching. Lots of them. Whoever it was, they had shown up just in time.

"Captain Lyndra, have you gone mad?" It was a young man speaking.

"Lord Finneus. So good to see you." The captain's tone made it clear she meant the exact opposite.

"Why are you tormenting my guests?"

"I have my reasons."

"You had best be prepared to explain them to Queen Avenel," the young man said. "In this city, she decides who lives and dies. You don't get to play judge, jury, and executioner."

"Thank you, Lord Finneus. I shall endeavor to remember that."

"Call your men off at once. We'll continue this conversation in the throne room."

Captain Lyndra issued a reluctant order in another tongue, and her men let Dean, Ronan, and Waverly go. The three of them traded looks of relief, thankful the forceful Lord Finneus (whoever he was) had come along when he did. A few more minutes with Lyndra and her men might have been the death of them, and for what? They hadn't even done anything wrong— as far as anyone knew. Dean was used to people trying to kill him, but they usually had their reasons. What Captain Lyndra's motives were, he couldn't hope to guess.

Dean and his friends turned around and came face to face with the young lord of Atlantis who had saved them. Dean was shocked; he couldn't have been more than fifteen years old.

"Honored visitors from the surface. I am Lord Finneus. You are now under my protection. Please accept my most humble apologies, and welcome to Atlantis."

CHAPTER 14

THE GREAT MACHINE

"Those maniacs nearly killed us," Waverly said.

"They will answer for that," Finneus promised. "Right now, I can only beg your forgiveness and ask that you allow me to greet you properly. On behalf of the royal family, it is my privilege to receive you. Whom do I have the honor of addressing?"

"My name is Waverly Kray. My friends are—"

"My lady," Finneus interrupted, bringing Waverly's fingers to his lips. "I am delighted to meet you." He looked up at Dean and Ronan. "Your friends as well."

"Delighted to be here," Ronan said.

Dean took a moment to size up Lord Finneus. The first thing

he noticed, apart from Finneus's youth, was the lord's skin color. Unlike Mookergwog and Lyndra, Finneus had pale, sky-blue skin. Most likely, he came from still another species of mer-people. He sported well-coiffed hair and wore a formfitting black suit— sleeveless, to show off his well-defined arms, and apparently cut from the hide of a manta ray. Glowing jewels were sewn into the shoulders and chest. Dean got the impression that Finneus was the kind of person who liked to spend a lot of time in front of the mirror.

"Who was that woman?" Dean asked, nodding toward Lyndra and her men.

"Captain Lyndra is Chief of Intelligence and Internal Security for Atlantis. Again, my apologies. She's suspicious of everyone. It's her nature. Those men were her personal guard."

"They were terrifying," Waverly said with a shiver.

"They originally hail from Abyssal, deepest city in the Mer-Realm. Formidable fighters, but brash and unpredictable. Very dangerous, the lot of them."

One of the soldiers Finneus had brought with him grunted. "Savages is what they are." He removed his helmet and showed off a thick scar running down the left side of his face. "I once nearly lost an eye over an innocent joke I made about one of their mothers."

"Some people have no sense of humor," Dean said.

"You're lucky we arrived when we did."

Dean looked at the scar-faced soldier. He and his comrades were the polar opposite of the Abyssian warriors, and for that matter of a different species than Finneus. They had fair skin—pale as Englishmen in winter—and wore thin, flexible golden armor. It looked like the kind of thing you could swim in—chain mail layered like fish scales, covering the soldiers from the waist up. They had golden helmets atop their heads with tight Y-shaped openings for their eyes, noses, and mouths. They also brandished long spears and held shields that bore a large capital *N*.

Finneus smiled uncomfortably. "Sir Riptide, please put your helmet back on." Finneus waited patiently as the man donned his helmet, hiding his scars once more. "These men here are from Neptune, the largest city in the Clearwater Kingdoms. No love lost between them and the people of Abyssal, I'm afraid."

"I can't imagine why," Ronan said.

"We had hoped for a warmer welcome," Waverly told Finneus.

"I pray you won't judge us based on this incident alone," Finneus said. "Truth be told, I'm disgusted that it happened. How can I make it up to you?"

"That's not necessary," Dean said. "We're fine. No harm done."

"On the contrary," Finneus began. "The laws of hospitality demand I make this right. I will not rest until you feel perfectly at home in Atlantis." He led the group into the city. "Consider me your tour guide. You must have a thousand questions. Ask away. I live to serve."

"We could start with the obvious," Ronan said. "How is it possible that we're walking on the ocean floor?"

"With air to breathe, no less?" Waverly added.

"And what is *that*?" Dean asked, unable to resist joining in. Up ahead, the central tower of a great castle reached up to touch the liquid shield that hung over the city. The dome-shaped waterfall covering Atlantis gushed out from the peak of the tower as if it were the centerpiece of an impossibly large fountain.

Finneus laughed. "*That* is the answer to all of your questions. A miracle of Atlantean science—the Water Tower."

Dean marveled at the sight. "I don't understand. It's just water that holds back the ocean?"

"Not just any water," Finneus corrected him. "Heavy Water. Many years ago, my ancestors discovered a Secret Sea beneath the ocean floor. It gets channeled up through the shaft of the tower and shot out through the fountain at the top. Gravity does the rest. As you can see, it mixes with the ocean about as well as oil and vinegar."

Everyone paused to admire the dome. Outside its walls, hundreds of rainbow-hued fish swam by. A handful of sharp-toothed predators chased after them, greedily snapping their jaws.

"Unbelievable," Ronan said. "I've sailed from one end of the Caribbean to the other. Seen things that would make a shark eat its own fin. But I've never seen anything like this."

"I envy you," Finneus replied. "I've been spoiled growing up here. The wonders of Atlantis are something I take for granted all too often."

"It's the most incredible thing I've ever seen," Waverly said. "A wondrous achievement."

"More than you know. Our royal engineers designed a process to constantly recycle the water through the system and pressurize the jet stream to cover the greatest possible distance. As if that wasn't enough, the Atlantean Alchemists' Guild created a process to extract oxygen from the water so that human visitors like yourselves can breathe."

Ronan tugged at his collar. "You mean if the machines in those towers fail, we'll run out of air?"

Finneus laughed again. "If the machines in those towers were to fail, we would have much bigger problems than that. The whole ocean would rain down upon us!" Waverly gasped. Finneus patted her arm. "Not to worry, my dear. The Tower has never once failed us. Not for a second."

Dean cleared his throat. "I notice you're breathing air, like us."

"We are partly amphibious, yes."

"Partly what?" asked Ronan.

"Mer-people are capable of breathing air *and* water," Finneus explained. "We just need to fully submerge our bodies once a day to keep ourselves hydrated."

"I don't understand," Waverly said. "Why go through the trouble of building your city this way if you don't need air to breathe?"

"It does seem an awful lot of work just to bring human entertainers down to the ocean floor," Dean agreed.

"Not at all. The number one business in Atlantis is tourism. Look around you, friends. The city is a melting pot. People come from every corner of the Mer-Realm to see our human attractions."

Sure enough, it was true. As they neared the city center, the streets got busier and people rushed to greet them at every turn. "Visitors!" they exclaimed. "Humans! Welcome to Atlantis!" The locals came in a variety of garments and skin tones. Some had fair, milk-white complexions like the Neptunian soldiers escorting them. Others were varying shades of blue (like Finneus), green (like Mookergwog), and gray (like the Abyssians).

"The highest purpose of Atlantis is to bring people together. Old enemies set aside ancient grudges to live here in peace. You see, at the heart of Atlantis is an idea: no matter how great our differences may be, deep down, we are all the same."

A few pale-skinned Neptunians balked at that lofty notion, the scarred Sir Riptide most of all.

"Some people in this pot take longer to melt than others, I see," Dean said.

Finneus grimaced. "My aunt likes to say that society is a great machine. One that does not always function as smoothly as the Water Tower."

"You must believe strongly in the principles this city was founded upon," Waverly said.

"I have to," Finneus replied. "As Minister of Cultural Exchange, it is my mission to see that every visitor is welcome in Atlantis."

"You're a minister?" Dean asked. "How old are you?"

"Don't make too much of my title. It's little more than royal nepotism. My aunt Avenel is the Queen, after all." They arrived at the gates of a great palace. "Here we are. I can't wait for you to meet her."

CHAPTER 15

THE QUEEN'S COURT

The queen's palace was the most impressive castle Dean had ever seen. It trumped even the Aqualine Palace of Zenhala, a feat he had not previously thought possible. A square-shaped outer wall with wide ramparts and stone parapets bordered the dwelling. Decorative pillars lined the exterior walls, leading up to a wide main gate with a heavy portcullis. Dean had seen those things before. It was the keep behind the gate that made him stop and stare: the central shaft of the Water Tower of Atlantis.

The structure took up nearly the entire courtyard and climbed a thousand feet into the air. It kept going and going, up and up and up, dominating the skyline of the city. Just looking at it—and the Heavy Water dome that flowed endlessly from the fountain at the top—made Dean feel small and insignificant. It was difficult not to feel that way in Atlantis.

Inside, Finneus led the group through a long central hallway lined with more columns. The walls were filled with stunning reliefs depicting two different armies swimming off to war. On the left wall, sharks, whales, and swordfish flanked noble Neptunians in handsome suits of armor. On the right wall, a furious stream of Abyssian warriors poured out from a crack in the ocean floor, followed by krakens, giant eels, and worse.

Up ahead, the scenes shifted to portray the two sides locked in combat. Dean, Ronan, and Waverly followed Finneus all the way down the hall, passing wall after wall of bloodshed and death.

"What is all this?" asked Waverly.

"Fascinating, isn't it?" said Finneus. "You are looking at the history of the Mer-Realm. Long before we were born, a great war was waged under the sea. It threatened to consume everything, but on this very spot, my grandfather—the first king of Atlantis—arranged a truce."

The hall opened into an antechamber where a pair of blue-skinned guardsmen stood before a massive door. Dean noticed one final scene above the portal, with the lords of Neptune and Abyssal bending their knees before a king on a shell-shaped throne.

"We've had a hundred years of peace," Finneus said. "People from both sides have shared this city the whole time. It isn't always easy. Visitors from Abyssal and Neptune don't always get along, but guests like yourselves provide some much needed diversion."

Finneus detached himself from Waverly to speak with the soldiers at the door. As they waited outside what could only be the queen's throne room, Dean's mind flashed back to a similar moment in the Aqualine Palace, waiting for Verrick to bring him before Waverly's father. Everyone had stayed in character that day. For Dean and his friends to be successful here, they would need the same level of focus.

"When should I ask about Gentleman Jim?" Ronan whispered.

"Not now," Dean hissed. "We're supposed to be world-famous entertainers invited by royal talent scouts. Just focus on that and keep quiet. I'll do the talking."

Finneus returned and the guards pulled the door open. Beyond the threshold lay a vast, bright chamber, all but empty. A gentle waterfall fountain trickled down the back wall and ran out across a raised platform, where the queen sat on her throne. The flowing water continued down a wide crystal staircase and then disappeared into a grate. Two guards in silver armor stood posted on either side of the queen's elevated seat, and two more waited at the base of the stairs with Captain Lyndra.

"This way," Finneus said, taking the first step toward the throne.

The group ascended the staircase to the royal dais, sloshing through running water as they went. Lyndra fell in line behind them, this time without her men. She eyed Dean and his friends with cold suspicion. When the group reached the top step, Finneus motioned for everyone to hold their position and continued on his own. Once he could go no farther without bumping into a guard, he stopped and took a knee. "We have visitors from the surface, my queen."

Queen Avenel, an old woman with long white hair and blue skin, wore a dress made of shimmery blue and white material, decorated with tiny seashells. The crown atop her head was a subtle, elegant coronet made of shining silver with three dazzling sapphires set inside it. Dean could tell the queen had been gorgeous in youth, for even now in her twilight years, she retained a graceful beauty.

"What a pleasant surprise," the queen smiled. "Captain Lyndra informed me I had guests, but she neglected to mention they were all so young."

"That's not all she hasn't told you," a voice called out from behind them. Dean turned around to see a thick man with a brown beard and the same garb as the soldiers of Neptune, with the addition of a shining golden cape. The man's temper appeared to rise off him like steam.

"I expect she also left out the part where her men nearly killed your guests upon arrival."

The queen was appalled. "Captain . . . is this true?"

Lyndra demurred. "Duke Shellheart exaggerates. I was merely questioning these children. They were in no real danger."

"No real danger?" Waverly said. "You threatened to drown us!"

Finneus rose. "I'm afraid that's true, my queen. Had I not arrived in time . . ."

The queen looked surprised. "You saved them, Finneus?"

"I commandeered a platoon of the duke's men to come to their aid." Finneus turned to the bearded man who had just joined them. "My apologies, Duke Shellheart. I did not mean to usurp your authority." Finneus then whispered an explanation to Dean and his friends: "The duke commands our royal navy."

Duke Shellheart grunted. "I will overlook it this once. Given the circumstances."

The queen aimed a punishing glare at Lyndra. "Explain yourself."

Lyndra appeared unfazed. "I was merely doing my duty for the good of Atlantis and the Mer-Realm as a whole. I have . . . concerns about these children."

"Based on what evidence?" Finneus asked.

"I have good reason to believe these children are not who they say they are."

"That doesn't exactly answer my question," Finneus replied.

Meanwhile, the hairs on the back of Dean's neck stood up. What had they done to arouse suspicion already? What detail had they overlooked?

"What are these reasons of yours, Captain? Tell me," said the queen.

Dean held his breath.

"I'm afraid I cannot divulge that information without compromising an ongoing investigation."

Finneus was incredulous. "What investigation? They just got here!"

Shellheart looked equally shocked. "You would refuse your queen?"

"In the purpose of protecting her, I must."

Shellheart scoffed. "This is outrageous. Your Majesty, if Captain Lyndra were under my command, I would never stand for such insubordination."

"I'm not under your command, Duke Shellheart," Lyndra coolly replied. "I serve at the pleasure of the queen."

"I can't imagine she derives any pleasure from your service. Your behavior is discourteous at best and treasonous at worst."

Lyndra turned on the duke with fire in her eyes. "You dare accuse me of treason?" She took a step toward Shellheart, her hand drifting back toward one of her knives.

"Ahem!" The queen cleared her throat, reminding everyone who was in charge. "I would like to hear from the children, who don't appear to be much of a threat to anyone. Tell me, are you the world-famous performers we have been told to expect or not?"

Dean stepped forward. "We are."

"And have you ever performed for a royal audience before?"

Dean nodded. "More than once. As a matter of fact, I was

recently booked in the court of the English king. They didn't want to let me leave."

"Wonderful. Tell me, what is it that you do?"

"What do we do?" Dean's stomach knotted. "Naturally, you would want to know that. It's an excellent question, Your Majesty. You honor us with the opportunity to introduce ourselves."

"Yes," the queen said. Dean's stalling did not go unnoticed. "Go on."

"Oh, nothing would please me more. We are . . . a variety show of sorts," Dean began, glancing at Waverly. "Daredevils!" he added. "A trio of world-class daredevils."

The queen was intrigued. "Do tell."

Dean beckoned Waverly. "Allow me to present the lovely and talented Waverly Kray. A more fearless cliff-diver you will not find, either above the sea or below."

"Is that so?" asked the queen.

Waverly looked sideways at Dean. "I do jump into things, Your Majesty. That much is true."

"From any height," Dean said. "Nothing fazes her."

"My court has never had the pleasure of viewing such a performance."

Waverly curtsied before the queen. "It honors me to be the first."

Dean tugged on Ronan's arm, directing him to stand beside Waverly. "Next, we have—"

"A fighter," Ronan cut in, pounding a fist into his palm. "I'm a fighter, born and bred."

Captain Lyndra chortled. "I highly doubt this boy is worthy of such a title."

"I'll fight anyone, anywhere, anytime," Ronan countered. "Ronan MacGuire, at your service, Your Majesty," he added, bowing his head.

"I look forward to seeing you in action," said the queen. "And what of you?" she asked Dean.

"Me? My own meager skills pale in comparison to those of my friends."

"Nonsense," said Waverly. "He's far too modest, Your Majesty. This one swims with sea serpents." She patted Dean on the back. "Isn't that right?"

"It is." Dean smiled enthusiastically, trying hard not to glare at Waverly. He had had something much less dangerous in mind for his performance.

"How exciting," said the queen, tapping her fingertips together. "Perhaps he'll be the one to receive Poseidon's blessing, eh, nephew?"

"I expect that is what Sir Fishback intended," Finneus said.

"Tell me, O tamer of wild sea serpents, what is your name?"

"Dean Seaborne, Your Majesty," Dean said with a bow. He wanted to ask what it meant to receive "Poseidon's blessing," but the queen had already moved on.

"Captain Lyndra," she said. "I realize you are only doing your job, but there is a line between protecting me and embarrassing me. These children are our guests. If they can do all that they have promised, would that quiet your concerns about them?"

"It would *help*," Lyndra allowed.

The queen aimed a playful smile at Dean. "I believe this is what people in your line of work call a 'tough crowd.' You had best live up to your billing, young man."

Dean smiled grimly. "Yes, Your Majesty."

"And, when we're done, will we really be paid in treasure?" Waverly asked.

"We shall keep our promises as well as you keep yours," the queen assured her. "Once you have dazzled my people with your rare talents and death-defying deeds, you'll be granted access to my vault. Do your jobs well, and you'll be permitted to leave with as much treasure as your little arms can carry. Fear not, I have far more than I could ever hope to spend."

"Are you quite sure of that, Queen Avenel?" Finneus asked.

The queen laughed. "My nephew thinks I'm going to live forever."

"One can hope," Finneus said.

The queen shifted in her seat. "Poseidon save me from such a fate. Duke Shellheart, Captain Lyndra . . . I expect to see you both at tonight's performance."

The Duke bowed his head. "Yes, my queen."

"I will be there," said Captain Lyndra.

"Good. Now, if there is nothing else?"

Ronan tapped Dean's shoulder. "Ask her now," he whispered.

Dean shook Ronan off. "Later!"

"What is it?" asked Queen Avenel, noticing their hushed squabble.

"There is one last thing," Dean said reluctantly. "We were hoping to find someone here. An old friend . . . His name was on the ledger in Aquatica."

"What name?" asked the queen, a trace of concern in her voice.

"Jim Harper," Ronan said.

The queen's eyes widened. She might have even gasped. Gentleman Jim's name had an effect on the room, and it was not a good one.

"We were told he opted to stay here after experiencing Atlantis," Dean said. He could sense everyone's apprehension, and his words came out sounding more like a question than a statement.

"That's not entirely accurate," Finneus said.

"He's not here, then?" Ronan said, crestfallen.

"Oh, he's here. He just didn't *choose* to stay . . ."

"I don't understand. Just tell me where to find him."

"Your friend's in prison," said Duke Shellheart.

Ronan straightened up with a jolt. "Prison! What for?"

Captain Lyndra's red eyes targeted Dean, Ronan, and Waverly with renewed vigor. "Murder."

CHAPTER 16

THE PRISONER OF
ATLANTIS

Finneus led Dean and his friends out of the throne room in
a huff.

"Just so we're clear, if you're friends with any other notorious
murderers in this city, I'd prefer you kept it to yourselves."

"I'm sorry," Dean said. "We didn't know he was accused of
murder."

"You should have asked me about your friend in private. Not
in front of the queen."

"You're right. We should have waited," Dean agreed, giving
Ronan a shove.

"How did you say you knew him?" Finneus asked. "Wait. Don't

answer that. Not here." He eyed the crowded halls of the palace.

"Can you take us to him?" Ronan asked.

Finneus sighed. "I might as well. The fish is already out of the net."

Gentleman Jim was being held at the outskirts of the city. Finneus led Dean, Ronan, and Waverley to his cell, a one-room stone hut right next to the Heavy Water barrier.

"In there," he said, pointing.

The building was colorless and depressingly small—the entire prison tinier than the room where Dean had been held captive back in Port Royal. His heart went out to Gentleman Jim. "How long has Jim been in there?"

"When does he get out?" Ronan added.

"*Will* he get out?" Waverly added.

Finneus shook his head. "He was taken into custody a week ago. As for when he'll be released . . . your friend was convicted of murder. The only way he's getting out of there is if he swims out."

"He's no murderer," Ronan said. "I know the man."

"Maybe he fell in with the wrong crowd," Waverly told Ronan. "Made a few bad decisions, trusted the wrong people . . . It happens."

Dean didn't like the way Waverly looked at them when she said that.

"I don't believe it," Ronan said. "I won't believe it. Not unless I hear it from Gentleman Jim's own lips."

"I expect you will soon enough," Finneus said. "He confessed to the crime once already."

The words hit Ronan like a cannonball to the stomach. "The devil, you say . . ."

"Surely there's been some mistake," Dean said.

"What'd you do, beat it out of him?" Ronan snarled. "Or maybe it was torture. Is that how you do things down here?"

Finneus's expression turned hard. "We did no such thing. Your friend came forward on his own. He hadn't even been a suspect."

Waverly, who knew Gentleman Jim by reputation alone, had less trouble believing Finneus's version of events. "Why'd he do it?" she asked.

"He wouldn't tell us that," Finneus said. "The victim was another friend of yours. Galen Fishback."

Ronan made a face. "We don't have any friends named—"

"The man who hired us?" Dean interjected. "We saw him only weeks ago," he added, frowning at Ronan.

"You won't be seeing him again," Finneus declared. "No one will. Sir Fishback was a good man. The city mourns his loss."

Ronan grunted. "I'm sure they do, but still . . . you have to admit there's something fishy about all this."

Finneus raised an eyebrow. "Fishy?"

"He means it doesn't make sense," Dean explained.

"I mean something stinks," Ronan said. "Why would he confess to murder but refuse to say why he did it?"

"You'll have to ask him," Finneus suggested. "Good luck with that. Your friend's a special brand of mystery."

They stopped outside the stone hut where Gentleman Jim had been locked up. It was so close to the Heavy Water barrier that the falls came down almost on top of it. Two blue-skinned Atlantean guards, clad in silver armor, stood watch on either side of the prison door.

"I can only permit you a few minutes alone with the prisoner. I'm sure you understand, a connection between you and our city's most infamous criminal isn't something I want to publicize. People will talk."

"We understand," Dean said.

Finneus snapped his fingers at the guards. "Open it up."

The guards unlocked Gentleman Jim's cell and stepped aside. Ronan, the first in line to enter, paused inside the doorway. "What in blazes?"

Dean and Waverly peered over Ronan's shoulder. They were shocked to find the rear wall of the cell was not a wall at all but rather a cascading torrent of Heavy Water.

"As you can see, this cell is specifically designed to hold a human," Finneus explained. Before the wall of Heavy Water, a man lay on a cot. He did not bother to turn around and greet his visitors.

"Did you build this cell just for him?" Dean wondered.

"Hardly," said Finneus. "Your friend isn't the first human to misbehave down here. Just the first one to earn himself a permanent residence. He'll spend the rest of his days here, assuming he doesn't opt to cut his sentence short."

"Cut his sentence short?" Ronan's face brightened. "How?"

"Ronan . . ." Dean motioned at the water. "The only way he's getting out is if he swims out, remember?" The cell teased its prisoner with an open door at back, testing the prisoner's desperation.

"Oh," Ronan muttered. "That's cold, mate."

"He did kill a man," said Finneus.

Ronan grunted. "We'll see about that."

Finneus withdrew and shut the door behind him as Ronan inched toward the man on the cot. The glowing crystal mountains beyond the city limits bathed the room in an undulating blue light.

"Hello?" Ronan called from across the room.

The prisoner spoke but did not stir. "Dinnertime already? Let me guess . . . more seafood."

"It's not dinner," Ronan said.

The man turned his head around halfway. "Who goes there?"

Ronan smiled. "I should think you'd recognize the voice of your own first mate. Or did you forget me already?"

"First mate?" The man stood up—Gentleman Jim Harper.

He was alive . . . but not necessarily well. The Gentleman Jim that Dean remembered was a strong, dashing, not-a-hair-out-of-place kind of man. The prisoner before him was scraggly and unkempt. *Everything* about him was out of place.

"What are you talking about?" the prisoner demanded. "Who are you? How do you know me?"

"Is this some kind of joke?" asked Dean.

"If it is, it's not funny. Cap'n, it's me. Ronan!"

Gentleman Jim strode up to Ronan and leaned in close to examine him. His frantic eyes darted this way and that as he studied Ronan's face.

"Seaborne . . . ," Ronan said, visibly uncomfortable.

Gentleman Jim's eyes shot upward. "Seaborne?" He looked at Dean as if Dean too were a stranger. He stared for a brief second, then shook his head and turned back to Ronan. The man seemed to be racking his brain, searching for some spark of recognition that refused to appear.

"No," he said at last. He turned away calmly, then erupted. "Blast it all!"

Gentleman Jim kicked the little cot he had been resting on. It went flying into the watery fourth wall of his cell, where the falls swept it away. Immediately regretting his outburst, Gentleman Jim balled a fist, seething. Dean, Ronan, and Waverly traded baffled looks, wondering what to say or do next. Gentleman Jim whirled on them.

"You're from the surface, like me," he said. His tone sounded like an accusation. Everyone nodded, open-mouthed. "This isn't some kind of trick . . . ," he continued. "You actually know me?"

A stilted breath rattled out of Ronan. "A trick? What are you . . . Of course we know you!"

Gentleman Jim nodded. "All right. Tell me." He motioned with his fingers like a man asking to be punched in the face. "Tell me who I am."

The room got deathly quiet. Ronan looked at Dean, dumbfounded.

"I'm confused," said Waverly. "Is it him or not?"

"It's him," Dean said, though he was no less confused than she was.

"Who?" Gentleman Jim demanded. "Come on, out with it!"

"You're Gentleman Jim Harper," Dean blurted out. "Captain of the *Reckless* and leader of the Pirate Youth."

Gentleman Jim blinked his eyes open. "A pirate? Really?"

"Of course, really!" Ronan said.

"I was a bad guy?"

Ronan looked offended. "Not at all. You were the only honest thief in the Black Fleet."

Gentleman Jim's eyes were the size of boiled eggs. "What are you talking about?"

"Don't you remember? It was you who thought up the Gentleman's Code."

"The what?"

"Your code! You made sure we only stole from people who could afford it, people who deserved it, or both."

"And I thought that made me a gentleman?" Gentleman Jim asked. He looked up at the ceiling. "That's got to be the most ridiculous thing I've ever heard."

"Ha!" Waverly laughed. "Thank you."

"You were all part of my crew?" Gentleman Jim asked.

"I wasn't," Waverly said. "I came later."

"Technically, Seaborne wasn't either," Ronan said. "He was a spy for the—"

"Ronan," Dean said. "Things are complicated enough already, don't you think?" He turned to Gentleman Jim. "How is it you don't know any of this? What did they do to you?"

Gentleman Jim sighed and rubbed his forehead like he had a migraine. "It wasn't anything they did. I came down here this way."

"Without your *memory*?" Ronan said.

Gentleman Jim nodded. "Must have left it topside. Just don't ask me where. I woke up three months ago on a ship full of strangers. When I looked in the mirror, the person I saw staring back at me was a stranger too." He rapped his knuckles against his temple. "My head was empty, except for one name. Gentleman Jim Harper. I've been waiting—praying—for the rest to come back to me, but I'm starting to wonder if it ever will. Three months later, I still don't know any more than I did that first morning."

"How does something like that even happen?" Ronan asked.

"He took quite a blow when our ship went down," Dean reminded Ronan.

Gentleman Jim's ears perked up. "Something hit me? What was it?"

"The mast," said Ronan. "A cannonball took it down. It swept the deck and sent you flying. If you hadn't pushed the two of us clear first, it would have killed us."

"So it's your fault I'm in this mess," Gentleman Jim said with the trace of a joker's grin.

Ronan winced. He didn't like hearing that, even in jest.

"How did you end up here?" Dean asked.

"Got lucky," Gentleman Jim said. "By all rights, I should be dead already. I was found floating along on a few battered planks of wood. Must have drifted for days. A company of actors fished me out of the sea. They were booked to perform at Aquatica, and ..."

"We understand how you got here," Waverly cut in. "We want to know how you got *here*." She motioned to Gentleman Jim's cell. "Did you kill Galen Fishback?"

Gentleman Jim stiffened. "You three came all the way down here to ask me that?"

"We came all the way down here to save you," Ronan said. "Captain's orders. No one gets left behind."

Gentleman Jim stroked his beard. He looked like he was about to speak further when the door swung open. Finneus walked in with an apologetic smile on his face. "I'm afraid your time is up," he said. "I hope this reunion went as well as possible, given the circumstances?"

"You didn't tell us about his condition," Dean said to Finneus.

"I thought perhaps your visit might jog his memory. Any luck?"

"None," Ronan said.

"I'm more interested in what he does remember," Waverly said. "He still hasn't told us. Did you kill Galen Fishback or not?"

Gentleman Jim spread his arms. "That's what I'm here for."

"That's not a yes," Dean said.

Gentleman Jim locked eyes with Dean. "Fine, then. Yes. I did that."

"Why?" Finneus asked, sounding as skeptical as Dean and his friends.

Gentleman Jim said nothing.

"I told you he was a special brand of mystery," Finneus complained.

Ronan addressed Gentleman Jim once more. "You're lying. I don't know why you are ... but you are."

Gentleman Jim shook his head. "You don't know that. You don't know me."

"More like *you* don't know you. I know ya just fine."

Gentleman Jim rested a hand on Ronan's shoulder. "I'm sorry ... Ronan. You seem a good lad. I wish I could remember you, but I can't. You should leave this place."

Ronan pushed Gentleman Jim's hand away. "It doesn't matter if you remember me or not. If you're in trouble . . ."

"*If* he's in trouble?" Waverly said.

Ronan leaned in close to Gentleman Jim and whispered, "I can't just leave you here."

"Of course you can," Gentleman Jim replied. "We're strangers, you and I. The man you knew is gone. At this point, I don't think he's ever coming back. Go home, all of you. Forget about me. If it helps, you can consider that my final order."

CHAPTER 17

A Friend in Need

"Go home, he says. Go home!" The reunion with Gentleman Jim had left Ronan red-hot. "As if I had one! The only place I ever called home was his ship. He's lost his bloody mind."

"Keep your voice down," Dean said, shushing Ronan. "Are you trying to blow our cover?"

"Yes, calm down," Waverly agreed. "At least, try. Eat something."

The queen's servants had prepared a sumptuous feast for the three of them. They sat alone in a great hall, before a dining table overflowing with food. A cornucopia of lobster claws, crab legs, oysters, clams, and shrimp had been spread out alongside tureens filled with hot butter and a large bowl of spicy red sauce.

"How can you eat at a time like this?" Ronan said.

"How can you not?" Dean said, taking a second helping of food. "I haven't had anything since yesterday. I'm starving."

"And while you're stuffing your face with shrimp, Gentleman Jim's locked up in a cell!" Ronan pushed his plate away and got up from the table. The pleasure of finding his former captain alive had given way to bitter frustration.

"I don't know what we can do to help him," Dean said discreetly. "We're going to have a hard time proving his innocence if he keeps confessing to the crime."

"You're assuming that he is innocent," Waverly said.

Ronan leaned over the table, steam coming out of his ears. "Mark me, and mark me well. He didn't do this. He's lying."

"Why would he lie about killing someone?"

"Could be he's protecting somebody," Dean offered.

"Or it could be he's telling the truth," Waverly said. "How do you know?"

"We know *him*," Ronan said.

"That's the problem," Waverly countered. "*He* doesn't. Maybe the Gentleman Jim you know isn't a killer, but the man he is now . . . the stranger in that cell? He might very well be. You don't know. You can't know."

Ronan gripped the back of his chair. Dean was certain he was going to pick it up and smash it against the wall, but Ronan surprised him by slumping down instead. "I want to hit somebody, but there's no one here to hit. I'm no good with this, Seaborne.

Making plans is your bailiwick. What are we going to do?"

"For now, we do nothing," Waverly said before Dean could answer. "And that means no more talk about it. The queen is expecting a show. We have to give her one. After that, we'll take our chests filled with treasure, use them to buy Verrick's freedom, and be done with it. That's it."

"I thought you didn't like that plan," Dean said.

"I don't," Waverly said. "What I'd *like* to do is ask Finneus to send a battalion up to the surface and help us retake the *Tideturner*, but it's too late to change our story now. And thanks to you two, we're friends with the city's most notorious criminal, which doesn't help our image as performers. You realize he killed the one person in Atlantis who could have exposed the three of us as frauds . . ."

Dean choked on a mouthful of lobster. He hadn't even thought of that.

"I don't see another way forward," Waverly continued. "We have to go through with this charade and hope that when it's over, we can buy Skinner off."

"What about Gentleman Jim?" Ronan asked.

Waverly looked at Ronan with pity in her eyes. "Ronan, I'm sorry. I know he meant a lot to you, and I know it pains you to lose him again, but he *is* lost. You said you wouldn't believe this of him until you heard it from his lips. Now you have. What more do you need?"

"I can't leave him in that cell, Waverly. He won't make it."

"Won't make it?"

"Put yourself in his position. Alone? Starin' at that wall of water, day after day? It's enough to drive a man mad. We leave him here with no hope, no reason to go on . . . he won't last a week."

"It's not just his life at stake, Ronan. Verrick's up there at the mercy of pirates, and they won't think twice about killing him. He took our place as their hostage, yours and mine. Would you leave him to die?"

The room was quiet. Ronan picked up a giant crab leg and gripped it until it snapped. He tossed away the cracked shell, still unable to eat.

"You have to choose. We can't save Gentleman Jim, but we can still save Verrick." Waverly rose from the table. "There isn't any time to waste. I'm going to ask Finneus if I can perform my act tonight. You two should be ready to go tomorrow at the latest."

Dean made a face like he'd just swallowed seawater.

"What's wrong?" Waverly asked.

"You had to tell them I swim with sea serpents?"

Waverly didn't see the problem. "What? It's nothing you haven't done before."

"With *one* sea serpent in Zenhala, and I was lucky to survive the experience! What makes you think I can just do that anywhere, anytime?"

"You told them we were daredevils. What was I supposed to say?"

Dean frowned. Clearly, the girl who risked her life for fun on a regular basis was not the best person to share his concerns with. Waverly left the room without another word. Dean stared at the door she left through. The distance between the two of them seemed to be growing by the hour. He felt as powerless to close the gap as he was to help Gentleman Jim. On the other side of the table, Ronan had laid his head in his hands. Dean couldn't think of anything to say that would make him feel any better, either.

"Hard to believe everything that's happened, these last few days."

Ronan looked up with weary eyes. "You can lay to that. How'd we end up in this mess?"

"Doesn't matter," Dean said. "We're here. In Atlantis," he added, still in disbelief. "It's funny. This is what we hoped for, the lot of us. Adventure. A chance to see the legends of the deep. I would've thought we'd enjoy it more."

Ronan laughed bitterly. "I hate to say it, but she's right. We're blasted lucky someone killed Galen Fishback. Otherwise, this caper would be over before it began."

"I don't think that was her point, but you're not wrong," Dean said. "Someone did us a favor on that score."

Ronan drummed his fingers on the table, deep in thought.

"I'm not leaving here without him, Seaborne. Don't bother trying to convince me otherwise."

"I don't think we have a choice. Verrick has two days to live, and today is half done. Not much time for us to play detective and clear Gentleman Jim's name, is there?"

"You're right. There isn't any time at all."

Dean squinted at Ronan. "So, what do you want to do?"

"I'll tell you what I *don't* want to do. I don't want to play detective. In fact, I don't care if he did it or not."

"What?"

"You heard me, Seaborne. I don't care. It doesn't change anything. Not a blasted thing."

"What are you saying?"

"I told you, I won't leave him behind. Not again. I don't want to clear his name. I want to break him out." Ronan slapped Dean on the back. "And you're going to help me do it."

PART FOUR

STUPID HUMAN TRICKS

CHAPTER 18

OPENING NIGHT JITTERS

Night had fallen in Atlantis. The crystal mountain range outside the city gave off a sleepy glow, but underneath the waterfall dome, excitement hung in the air. It was showtime at the palace.

Queen Avenel's castle sat at the head of a public square in the middle of the city. Dean, Ronan, and Waverly were there along with at least a thousand others, mermen and mermaids who filled the long rows of gallery seats provided for the occasion. Half the city had turned out to see the famed human circus and witness the wonders of the surface world. Vendors roamed the stands, selling food and souvenirs. At the edge of the plaza, a band played loud, lively music while the audience waited for the show to begin. Children bounced eagerly in their seats, giggling and gawking at Dean, Ronan, and Waverly as if the trio were an odd zoological exhibit.

At least they're happy to see us, Dean thought. He longed to share the crowd's enthusiasm, but the fates of Verrick and Gentleman Jim weighed on his mind like an anchor. Try as he might, he couldn't see a way clear to saving both men. They weren't the only ones in danger, either.

"You're sure you want to go through with this?" Dean asked Waverly.

They were standing at the base of a tower that had been built in the middle of the square. A thin ladder ran up the side of the newly erected frame to a wooden plank high up in the air. If the masts of three ships had been stacked up, one on top of the other, they would have still fallen well short of the diving board's height.

"Waverly?" Dean asked again, pressing her for an answer.

Waverly clutched at the collar of a robe she had on over her clothes and took a deep breath. That was it. She didn't gulp, shiver, or shake. If Waverly was scared, she wasn't going to show it. "Don't worry about me," she said. "You've got enough to worry about on your own, I think."

Dean scowled. She didn't know the half of it. He had deliberately not told Waverly about Ronan's desire to spring Gentleman Jim from prison.

"How are you supposed to do any cliff-diving in this plaza?" Dean asked, changing the subject. "Aren't we missing something?"

He gestured to the open space below the diving board. There was no water at the landing spot, only an empty platform.

"Not to worry," Finneus called out. "If there's one thing we never lack for in Atlantis, it's water." He arrived with Duke Shellheart and a contingent of soldiers, all of whom came from Neptune. "What do you think?" Finneus asked, waving to the vibrant crowd.

"Quite a turnout," Waverly said.

"I expected nothing less," Finneus replied.

"I'm impressed you were able to put this evening together so quickly," said the duke. "I expect you wanted to get a human back on stage as soon as possible. Helps to takes everyone's mind off the one who was just on trial."

Finneus grimaced. "This group of performers will be more to your liking, I assure you. More to everyone's liking."

The duke gave a dubious grunt. "The queen is expecting me."

Shellheart went to join Queen Avenel in her royal box. "Everyone's a critic," Finneus muttered as he left.

Dean spied Captain Lyndra sitting next to the queen, looking every bit as fierce as he remembered. Lyndra's personal guard, a squad of eight armored Abyssians, stood at attention nearby. Both she and the duke surrounded themselves exclusively with their own countrymen. It struck Dean that neither one of them seemed on board with the great experiment of Atlantis. *Maybe in another hundred years*, Dean thought.

"It's time," Finneus announced to Waverly. "I'll introduce you. It's part of my duties as master of ceremonies this evening."

Waverly nodded. "I'm ready."

"Good luck. Not that you need it," Finneus said with a wink.

The crowd cheered as Finneus made his way over to the platform beneath the diving board. The evening's entertainment was set to begin at last. The young lord's voice came booming across the square, impossible to ignore.

"Ladies and gentlemen, boys and girls! May I have your attention, please?" He was speaking into a large cone-shaped seashell that amplified his voice. Acting as the ringleader, he quieted the crowd in an instant.

"Thank you, one and all. Thank you for coming tonight! It is our great pleasure, as always, to have you with us in Atlantis, shining jewel of the Mer-Realm. The court of Queen Avenel is proud to once again bring you the greatest show under the sea!"

The crowd roared.

"Many of you have come a long way to be with us this evening, to experience the wonders of the surface world. And here in Atlantis, we do not disappoint." He threw his own hand out, presenting Waverly to the assembled masses. "I give you the lovely and talented daredevil diver—*the utterly fearless*—Waverly Kray!"

Waverly waved to the adoring crowd, sporting a one-piece swimsuit covered in silver and gold sequins for the festivities.

Dean and Ronan joined the audience in applauding her. They were background players this evening.

"Tonight, as part of an exclusive, limited-run engagement, London's princess of peril will demonstrate the bravery and skill that separates her from other surface-dwellers, as she risks her life in a dive from one hundred feet in the air"—Finneus motioned to the diving tower—"into *this* pool of water."

Finneus pointed to a team of mermen who were carrying out a tank of water hardly bigger than a barrel. The crowd *ooh*ed and *aah*ed.

"That?" Dean said. "You're diving into *that?*"

The pool was not worthy of the name. Waverly went on smiling brightly, unfazed by its miniscule size. Dean realized she had known all about this little twist. She had already agreed to it.

"Waverly, are you crazy? You can't do this. It's too dangerous."

She smirked. "You sound like my father."

"I'm serious," Dean said.

"So am I. You sound just like him."

"Are you trying to get yourself killed?" asked Ronan.

"More like I'm trying to *keep* someone from getting killed. Now, wipe those terrified looks off your faces. This is supposed to be an act we do all the time."

Dean swallowed his pride and put on a wooden smile as Finneus rejoined them.

"Shall we, my lady?" Finneus asked Waverly, offering his arm.

"We shall."

Finneus helped Waverly up onto the first rung of the ladder and asked the audience to give her one more round of applause as she began her ascent. No two ways about it, Dean thought— Waverly *did* have a death wish. It was one thing to be daring, but this was plain crazy. Even if the water were deep enough to dive into—which it wasn't—the tank was still so tiny. Aiming for such a small mark from such a height allowed Waverly zero margin for error. She had to score an exact bull's-eye. Anything less, and they'd be mopping her off the floor.

"She's out of her mind," Dean said.

"You're just finding that out now?" Ronan asked.

The band played a long drumroll while Waverly climbed the ladder. The crowd fell silent as the endless *rat-a-tat* filled the plaza. Dean's heart inched farther into his throat with every step she took.

By the time Waverly took her place at the top of the tower, Dean could hardly see her. And, surely, the water tank was no bigger than a coin from Waverly's point of view. The drumroll stopped, and dead silence followed. Time stood still as Dean hoped Waverly would turn around, refusing to go through with the dive—but he knew it wasn't in her to back out. Time sped up again as she dove out into the air.

She fell.

One hundred feet straight down, she held perfect form as she flew spiraling toward the water. Dean only wished she could fly.

From his vantage point, he couldn't see if she was on course or not. For all Dean knew, her life was already over. He held his breath, praying she would hit the mark.

She entered the water with the tiniest of splashes, disappearing into the barrel-sized pool in the blink of an eye. Another pause followed, feeling like an eternity.

Waverly popped her head out of the water with a hand in the air and a smile on her face. The band sounded triumphant horns at the sight of her, and the crowd went wild. Everyone in the plaza, including the queen, got to their feet and lauded her death-defying stunt. As the people stomped and whistled and showered Waverly with applause, Dean finally exhaled.

He and Ronan ran to the water tank. Waverly was still inside, waving to the crowd and blowing out thank-you kisses, intoxicated by the thrill of the moment. She splashed water playfully at Dean and Ronan as they closed in on her.

"That was incredible!" Ronan exclaimed.

"Amazing!" Dean added. He walked around the tank, unable to make sense of what had just happened. "How did you do that? This water isn't deep enough!"

"Are you sure about that?"

Dean pushed at the base of the tank. "I don't understand. Is it resting over a well?"

"Have a closer look." Waverly shot her arms out and pulled Dean into the water.

Before Dean knew what was happening, he was going in headfirst. He fell into the pool, expecting to be smushed next to Waverly, but there was plenty of room. He flipped around easily inside the tank. A wide expanse of water, impossibly deep and infinitely vast, stretched out before him. It seemed to somehow go on forever.

No wonder Waverly wasn't worried, Dean thought. *It's more enchanted water, like the Waterways that took us to Atlantis. She knew she was jumping into a portable ocean.*

Dean swam for the surface and emerged to find Ronan laughing at him.

"I told you I'd be fine," Waverly said.

Dean splashed a little water her way. "You knew about this. This water."

"They call it DeepWater. And of course I knew about it. I'm not crazy."

Dean's lips curled up in a crooked smile. "Sometimes I wonder."

"Bravo!" Finneus said, beaming. "They love you. I knew they would. Look, you even won over Lyndra and Shellheart!"

As Finneus helped Waverly out of the tank, Dean looked to the royal box. It was true. Captain Lyndra was actually clapping. She seemed pleasantly surprised.

"You're a hit," Dean told Waverly.

"Truly an awe-inspiring performance," Finneus said. He

turned to Dean. "I think your act is the only one capable of following it!"

The smile drained away from Dean's face. "About that . . . Is it really possible for me to go swimming with a sea serpent down here?" He fervently hoped the answer was no.

"More than possible," Finneus replied. "It's perfect. Especially for you."

"Why do you say that?"

"Because . . ." Finneus leaned against the edge of the pool and lowered his voice to a whisper. "I know who you really are and what you're planning to do."

CHAPTER 19

Partners in Crime

Finneus refused to say any more in the plaza. "Too many people around. We'll talk later," he had said in a voice too low for Dean's friends to hear.

After the show, Waverly returned to the palace to put on some dry clothes. Dean and Ronan headed to the public house where they'd agreed to meet Finneus, and the majority of people who had watched Waverly's dive had similar destinations in mind. As Dean and Ronan walked the streets, they found the city alive with energy. They passed several packed taverns and inns, finally stopping at the largest of them all. The sign above the door read *Undercurrents*. Loud music and louder voices poured out from within.

"This is where he wants to meet?" Ronan asked.

Dean nodded. "This is it. Undercurrents. Certainly sounds like the kind of place where the criminal element would meet up."

"Question is, who told him that's *our* element?"

"It's not our element. Not anymore."

"Let's hope we can convince him of that."

They started toward the door. The line of people waiting to get in ran around the corner, but everyone stepped aside to let them pass. People stared in wonder as Dean and Ronan went by. They were celebrities.

The great room of the tavern was vast and filled with long tables that were packed with people. The barkeeps and serving maids ran around, trying to keep everyone's glasses full. Dean and Ronan spotted Finneus in the back of the room, waving them over.

Dean was worried about what Finneus knew and, more importantly, what the young lord was going to do about it. If their cover was truly blown, the smart thing for Dean and his friends to do was cut their losses and run, but they couldn't do that. Not with Gentleman Jim still in prison and no safe harbor to return to above the sea. Dean didn't even know how to get back to the surface without help. No two ways about it—he had to meet with Finneus.

"Maybe he was bluffing," Ronan said as they walked to his table. "Fishing for information?"

"Didn't feel like it," Dean said.

"But how could he know we mean to break Gentleman Jim out of prison? We haven't even told Waverly."

"You want to say that a little louder, Ronan? There might be one or two people in here that didn't hear you."

Ronan bit his lip. He had answered his own question—someone must have heard them talking about it back in the palace.

"We've been sloppy since we got here," Dean said. "Can't afford that. Let me do the talking with Finneus, all right?"

Ronan motioned to the young lord of Atlantis, seated at a private table with a pretty young mermaid. "He's all yours."

"There you are!" Finneus called out. "About time." He turned to the girl sharing his table. "I'm sorry, dear, but duty calls. My human friends and I have important matters to discuss."

"You work too hard," the mermaid replied, pouting as she rose from the table.

"The work of a minister is never done," Finneus replied. He motioned for Dean and Ronan to take the vacant seats around his table. "Please, join me. Can I offer you gentlemen a drink?"

"We're fine." Dean sat down. "You didn't ask us here to drink."

"Right to business, then. A man after my own heart."

Dean scanned the area around the table. He saw no armored Atlanteans. Despite the looks Dean and Ronan had received from passersby outside, no one at Undercurrents seemed to be paying much attention to them at all.

Finneus leaned into Dean's line of sight. "What are you looking for?"

"Guards."

"You won't find any in here. We still have to watch what we say, of course."

"I'm not sure what there *is* to say," Dean said. "I don't know what you think we're planning to do, but—"

"Let me stop you right there," Finneus said, cutting Dean off. "We both know you aren't world-famous daredevils."

Dean put on his best poker face and prayed that Ronan was capable of doing the same. He didn't have the heart to look.

"Don't worry, your secret's safe with me," Finneus assured them. "This city runs on tourism. Killer humans are bad for business," he added with a wink.

Ronan's back stiffened. "Jim Harper's no killer. He didn't murder Galen Fishback. He couldn't have."

"I know that," Finneus replied.

Dean and Ronan shook in their seats.

"That's why the three of us are talking," Finneus continued. "I didn't ask you here to arrest you, if that's what you're wondering. Quite the opposite. I'm going to make your job easier."

"*What?*" Dean and Ronan both said at once.

"You heard me. I want to help you."

Ronan leaned over the table. "You mean to tell me you're actually going to—"

"Quiet," Finneus said as a barmaid swooped in with a round of bright green drinks. Ronan clammed up straightaway.

Dean sat in stunned silence, trying to make sense of Finneus's offer. *The queen's nephew wants to help us free Gentleman Jim? Am I hearing things?*

"These are on the house," the barmaid announced, setting down three glasses. "It's the least we can do. After all, your friends from the surface are the reason we're so busy. I was worried we wouldn't have a night like this for quite some time."

"And why is that?" asked Finneus.

"No offense, my lord, but after what happened to Sir Fishback, I simply assumed these shows were done for. We all did."

Finneus laughed. "Not to worry, my dear. By this time tomorrow, Fishback's killer will be a distant memory." He pointed at Dean. "This one's going to swim with the eels of Lightning Canyon."

The barmaid's eyes widened. "Really?"

"He wanted it to be sea serpents," Finneus explained. "I'm afraid that's easier said than done. Getting a sea serpent in here would be a feat in and of itself. But giant eels, as you know, are native to the area. We can go to them. Far more manageable, really."

The barmaid was clearly impressed. "Lord Finneus, I don't know where you find these people, but you've outdone yourself with this batch. Every innkeeper in Atlantis will be singing your praises."

"Not mine. Theirs." Finneus pressed a gold coin into the girl's palm. "I am but a humble facilitator of culture and commerce."

The barmaid thanked Finneus and left the table. Dean squinted at the young lord. "Giant eels? What are you doing?"

"My job. People expect me to talk about your upcoming performance."

"You just said you thought we weren't daredevils."

"I know you're not," Finneus said. "We still have to keep up appearances, don't we?"

"Stow appearances," Ronan said. "Explain to me what Gentleman Jim's still doing in jail if you know he's innocent."

"You think I want him there? The man confessed." Finneus twirled a finger at his temple. "His mind isn't right. Nothing I can do for him. All I can do is help you."

"By putting me in the water with giant eels?" Dean asked.

"By putting you right where you need to be."

Dean leaned back from the table. "You've lost me."

"I'll explain. Have you ever heard of the Blood of Poseidon?"

Dean thought about it. "Actually, I have. Mookergwog mentioned it back at Aquatica."

"What did he say?"

"He was going on about how Atlantis is home to three of the Seven Great Wonders of the Mer-Realm. The Water Tower, which we've already seen. The Magic Mountains, which I expect is the glowing mountain range around the city. And then there was the Blood of Poseidon. But he didn't say anything more about it."

"The Blood of Poseidon is the rarest substance on earth," Finneus said. "And the most sacred—bestowed upon Atlantis by the sea god himself. It's why this city is the capital of the Mer-Realm. We keep it in a special chamber beneath the castle, the same place in which we harvest the Heavy Water. Only the queen is allowed to enter. Not even her guards are permitted, but you, Dean Seaborne . . . you will be granted access in the morning."

"What for?" Dean asked.

"To receive the sea god's blessing. The Blood of Poseidon is a transformative elixir. A single drop turns man into merman and vice versa. Temporarily, of course."

Dean's jaw dropped. "You're going to make me like you?"

"It's tradition. The transformation is symbolic of the queen's desire to break down barriers. One human from every visiting party gets the chance to experience life through our eyes. Your act makes you the obvious choice—and gives you the opening you need to carry out your plans."

The wheels in Dean's head turned fast. *Your plans.* Gentleman Jim's prison was mostly water. If Dean could swim like a fish—*as a fish*—that changed everything. There were no guards on the ocean side of Gentleman Jim's cell. They could get Jim out that way. And with help from Finneus, they could get him home. It seemed too good to be true.

"Why are you helping us? What's your interest here?"

Finneus sipped his drink. "I think that should be obvious."

Dean studied Finneus. He thought about the packed restaurants, taverns, and inns he and Ronan had passed on their walk through the city. The barmaid had feared that Gentleman Jim's infamy might drive away customers, or worse, shutter visits from human performers altogether. It was a problem Finneus would surely have loved to be rid of.

"What about afterward?" Dean asked Finneus. "What then?"

"After is easy. You get your money and you leave."

"*With* Gentleman Jim," Ronan stressed.

Finneus made no objections. "Why not? I've no use for the man."

"Your people won't be nervous about an 'escaped killer' on the loose?"

"You've seen his cell. People will think he gave up. Wandered into the ocean." Finneus fluttered his fingers like a minnow riding the current. "Out of sight, out of mind. Extraordinary coincidence that you should know him, by the way. Almost impossible to believe."

"I've said the same thing fifty times since we got here," Dean replied.

"Aye," Ronan grunted, "now you know how we feel."

"What about the girl you're with? Waverly. Is she a part of this?"

"She doesn't know anything about it," Dean said. "Doesn't much care to know either."

"Fair enough. She won't hear it from me," Finneus promised. "In fact, I don't want to know any more myself. I'll leave the details up to you two."

"Not a problem," Dean said.

"Good." Finneus looked around and spotted the girl he had been talking to earlier. He rose from the table, taking his drink with him. "We're finished here, gentlemen. You two should get some rest. Tomorrow's going to be an exciting day."

Outside the tavern, Ronan could barely contain his excitement. It took everything he had to wait until they were on a quiet street before he grabbed Dean's shoulder.

"Seaborne, am I dreaming?" he asked, shaking Dean. "Did that really just happen? Finneus basically said he'd let us walk off with Gentleman Jim!"

"Easy now." Dean pushed Ronan off before he broke his shoulder. "Don't go celebrating just yet. If Finneus is right, I can get through his cell's water wall with the Blood of Poseidon. That doesn't help Gentleman Jim get out. After my performance, we'll need to sneak back into wherever it is they keep the blood and steal an extra dose of the stuff for him."

"That ought to be easy enough. Finneus said they don't let

anyone down in the chamber—not even the guards. Just keep your eyes peeled when you're there with the queen and find us a way in. Nothing to it."

"Nothing to it," Dean repeated. "Assuming I survive the eels."

Ronan grimaced. "Right. Sorry, mate. I forgot about that part."

CHAPTER 20

BLOOD FROM A STONE

It seemed that only one person in Atlantis didn't want Dean to swim with the eels. One person other than Dean, that is.

"Your Majesty, I must object to this," Lyndra told the queen.

Dean sighed. *Why am I not surprised?*

On the morning of his performance, Dean and Lyndra stood in the throne room with Queen Avenel, her guards, and a collection of royal stewards and handmaids. Finneus had already seen Ronan and Waverly off to Lightning Canyon, where they would watch from the safety of a pod. Dean was the lone human in the room . . . for the moment. Soon, he would grow flippers and gills just like his hosts, but not until after Lyndra had her say. Again.

The queen was patient in the face of Lyndra's dissent.

"Captain, we've been through this already. I would have thought that last night put your suspicions to rest."

"About the girl, perhaps," Lyndra said.

"Very good. And now we shall give the boy his own turn to prove himself. And what better way than by delivering the sea god's blessing? It's one of my favorite traditions. You know that."

"Yes, Your Majesty, but—"

"But nothing," the queen said. "The rite of transformation represents all that Great Poseidon asks of us. To open our minds and embrace each other's cultures without reservation. To surrender our narrow viewpoints and see the world with new eyes. The opportunity to do that is what makes Atlantis special."

"Queen Avenel, I cherish the tradition as well, but I fear for your safety. This Seaborne—"

"Is a child," said the queen.

"A child who may be involved in a plot against you."

Dean couldn't help himself. "What are you talking about? Finneus said you were suspicious by nature, but this . . . you can't be serious."

Captain Lyndra's crimson eyes bored into Dean. "Deadly serious."

"You said involved in a plot," the queen stated. "Involved with whom?"

Lyndra shook her head. "My queen, I don't dare name my suspects without proof."

"But you have no problem accusing me," Dean complained.

"You are a stranger here."

"He is a *guest*," the queen said, chastising Lyndra with her eyes. Her point made, Queen Avenel smiled at Dean. "The good captain forgets her manners only out of concern for my well-being. Her heart is in the right place, I am sure."

"Mine is too," Dean said. "You've nothing to fear from me, Your Majesty."

"Of course not. I've administered this rite more times than I can count. No harm will come to me under the watchful eye of the sea god."

"If you would but allow me and my men to accompany you," Lyndra began.

"Soldiers in the chamber of Poseidon?" The queen shook her head. "You know better than that, Captain." She motioned for Dean to join her. "Come, young man. Crowds have been gathering at the canyons all morning to see you swim with the eels. We mustn't keep the public waiting."

Before Dean could move forward, Lyndra caught him by his elbow. "Know this, *daredevil*. Whatever happens, I'll be seeing you again. You'd best behave yourself."

Dean pulled himself free of Lyndra's grasp. Her fingers were like ice. Everything about her gave Dean the chills.

He followed the queen to the waterfall of a wall behind her throne. Two of her guards stuck their shields into the falling water, and the arch they created revealed a doorway. "This way," said the queen as she stepped inside. Everyone else stayed behind as Dean and Queen Avenel entered the secret passageway.

"Blow me down," Dean whispered, shielding his eyes as he followed the queen inside. Just behind the wall, in a room that was as bright as day, lay the Atlantean treasure vault. It was as big as the hold of a ship. Heaping mounds of gold stood before Dean, piled high like sand dunes on a beach. Sconces filled with glowing crystals from the Magic Mountains had been placed throughout the room, and their cool, steady light reflected off an endless supply of silver coins, rubies, diamonds, and pearls. Dean had never before glimpsed such a display of wealth. Zenhala's golden orchard—even in full bloom—could not have compared.

Three chests full of this, he thought. That's what they had been promised. Now that Dean had seen Queen Avenel's trove, he knew it would be enough to buy Verrick's freedom. Three chests would be enough treasure to satisfy the greediest pirates alive, just so long as they didn't know how much Dean had left behind.

He followed the queen down a winding stone path in between the rolling hills of treasure, dizzied by the sight of the royal fortune.

"Don't forget to blink," Queen Avenel said. "If you're not careful, your eyes might fall out of your head."

Dean ran a hand through his hair. "I've never seen so much gold in one place."

"It's pretty to look at, of course, but gold by itself serves no real purpose. For something truly priceless, we must go deeper."

They left the vault, moving down a metal staircase that wound its way around a massive copper tank. Wires, hoses, pipes, and gauges were scattered across the face of the tank. Dean slid his hand across it as he descended the steps. The copper tank was cool to the touch and as big as a boat. He realized he was standing beside the source of the Heavy Water that separated Atlantis from the ocean. Its contents would soon be sprayed out from the very top of the Water Tower. Dean and the queen pressed on. Farther down, Dean heard rushing water and saw what looked like fog clouds, but could not see the bottom of the chamber.

"How much deeper can we go? Aren't we already at the bottom of the ocean?"

"This place is home to deeper mysteries than you can possibly fathom. You'll see."

When they finally reached the bottom of the water tank, the staircase gave way to a vast cavern. Glowing crystals grew out of the wall in spiky protrusions, lighting the area. Huge waterfalls, the size of tidal waves, poured out from decorative fountainheads in the cavern walls. Torrents of viscous, oil-like water cascaded down the sides of the chamber, sending white, cloudy vapors upward. Dean waved his hands in front of his face to clear his vision. Below him, the waterfalls turned massive turbines that powered the machinery of the tower, then continued back out to sea through a tunnel at the base of the chamber.

Queen Avenel gestured to the rushing water. "That is how you will leave this place . . . with Poseidon's blessing, of course," she added.

At the very bottom of the staircase was a metal grate platform, anchored to the base of the water tank. Dean stepped onto the platform and looked through the misty fog. There was someone waiting out at the edge of the platform.

"That isn't . . . Poseidon?" asked Dean. Could it be he was about to meet the fabled sea god?

The queen said nothing.

Dean walked toward the man in the mist. Once he got close enough, he saw that it was not a person at all, but a statue. A cobalt blue mineral had grown across the floor like algae. At the edge of the platform, the blue stone had been carved in the image of Poseidon—more than seven feet tall, with powerful muscles. In one hand, he held his signature weapon and symbol of power, the trident. He held out his other hand in a welcoming gesture. A milky-white liquid leaked out from a crack in the wrist of this outstretched hand. It dripped down into a goblet at the base of the statue, one extremely slow drop at a time.

"What you see before you is the power behind my throne," the queen told Dean. "My kingdom is much smaller than Neptune and Abyssal, but Atlantis has held Poseidon's favor ever since my father first built the city. The mineral from which we carved this statue grew in this chamber after construction was complete. We believe Poseidon saw what we had created here and smiled upon our efforts. That is why Atlantis alone was given the power to end Abyssal and Neptune's great war."

Dean studied the strange milky liquid leaking out from the stone. "Ending the war . . . How did the Blood of Poseidon do that?"

"By lending us the sea god's might. If you touch this potion, you will be transformed. But if you drink it and Poseidon deems you worthy, you gain dominion over every fish in the sea. An endless, unstoppable navy. My father was the first to wield this power. Once the rulers of Neptune and Abyssal understood its depths, they had no choice but to accept the truce he enforced."

A lone drop of Poseidon's blood fell into the goblet.

"In His wisdom, Lord Poseidon gives His gift sparingly. Every month, when this glass is full, I must drink from it or else lose control over the denizens of the deep. But I am glad to spare a few drops for you today. The miraculous transformation you are about to undergo is a reminder to all that the sea god's power is real and that I am his instrument here on Earth. That knowledge helps keep the peace under the sea."

"The peace is that fragile? After a hundred years?"

"That is the nature of peace," the queen said. "We must fight to keep it, always. But without fighting."

"What was the great war even about?"

The queen grimaced. "Nothing worthwhile, I'm afraid. People have their differences. Different customs, traditions, skin tones . . . Some people hardly need any reason at all to go to war. We have to show them another way. That's why we invite humans like you to Atlantis. It's the same reason my court and council is made up of mer-people from across the sea, including Neptune and Abyssal. There is wonder to be found in people who are nothing like us, and much to learn."

The queen picked up the goblet of Poseidon's sacred blood. "This is the real treasure of my kingdom," she said. "That which brings us together and helps us see that we are all the same. Distance and isolation breed mistrust. Fear. Contempt. Visitors like you help me turn back such foes." She withdrew a silver wand from her robe. "The Blood of Poseidon can change you for a day, a week, a year . . . even permanently, depending on the portion you receive. You shall be granted enough to swim in the fins of a merman for a day. Do you accept the sea god's gift with an open mind and an open heart?"

Dean's eyes swept the chamber, looking for a way to sneak in later. He found one.

"I do," he said.

And I'll be back for more.

"I must warn you. Most humans find the transformation disorienting at first. Your new body will cry out for water. You must take to the sea at once. Finneus will be waiting outside to bring you to Lightning Canyon."

Dean took a breath. "I'm ready."

I think.

Queen Avenel dipped the wand into the goblet and flicked a smattering of the magic potion at Dean. He flinched as if scalded, but the blood's touch did not burn. It froze him to the marrow.

As the Blood of Poseidon traveled through his pores and began mingling with Dean's own blood, he felt his lungs ice over and shrivel up inside his chest. Everything inside of him was cold, as if a glacier had materialized inside his body.

The soft glow of the crystal spurs nearby attacked Dean's eyes like daggers of brilliant light. All of his senses had been amplified. Next came a searing pain on the back of his jawline, like someone was cutting him behind the ears. Then, in an instant, it was over. He felt fine. No more cold. No more pain. Just a thirst. One that went beyond anything he had ever experienced before. He opened his mouth to breathe, but nothing happened. He began to stagger around, suffocating and helpless.

"To the sea!" said the queen. "To the sea! You need water!"

Dean turned to the heavy streams racing out of the cavern. He backed up a few paces and then ran hard for the edge of the platform. A primal need was driving him. Instinct. He hit the edge and dove out, arms outstretched. A second later, he plunged into the jet of water and breathed deep as the current pulled him under and away.

CHAPTER 21

Treacherous Depths

Dean kicked off his boots as he swam, going limp like a fish, bending this way and that as he followed the current's swirling path. It was a relief to be in the water. He felt at home there, completely at peace. He had hardly noticed his new webbed feet. Dean closed his eyes and let the sea carry him, trusting the tide would take him where he needed to go.

The flowing water deposited him in a cool, dark stretch of ocean outside the city. As he drifted to a halt, Dean noticed the light of Atlantis's large glowing mountain range in the distance. He was on the other side of the Magic Mountains.

Dean waved his arms and kicked his feet in the water, trying to get a sense of up and down. He felt lightheaded and punchy as he adjusted to his new body, with too many thoughts and sensations to process at once. The ocean was cold and dark, but the chill didn't bother Dean as much as it should have. Was he cold-blooded now? Most fish were, weren't they?

Dean swam in circles, trying to remember what it was he had to do. He knew the task was something dangerous, but he wasn't scared anymore. Not like he had been. He turned his body, flipping around gracefully. His reflexes were already growing sharper, his movements becoming automatic. Dean laughed at the realization that he was breathing underwater and it had taken him this long to notice. His metamorphosis was complete—and completely remarkable.

Dean felt as if the ocean were a dance partner he had trained with for years. He swam like a fish—even better than a fish, and with no more than a minute of experience as a merman. He was in his element. Nothing could touch him down here unless he wanted it to. Swimming in his new body, he wasn't worried about sea serpents, giant eels, or anything else in the deep blue sea.

Ripples in the water alerted Dean to someone nearby. By the time he turned to see who was there, Finneus was already upon him. "Easy now, I've got you," the young lord said, taking hold of him by the shoulders.

The queen had told him her nephew would be waiting outside to guide him to the canyons, Dean remembered. That was why he was there—to swim with the eels of Lightning Canyon.

"Is it done?" Finneus asked.

Dean remembered his mission too, but he was still disoriented from his transformation and struggled to speak while fully submerged.

"Don't worry, we can talk here," Finneus said, gently coaxing him. "Is it done?"

"No," Dean gurgled. "Not yet."

"Not yet?" Finneus's mood shifted drastically. "What do you mean, not yet?"

Dean shook his head, still a bit woozy. "I couldn't. The queen was right there."

"Of course she was there. That was the point!"

"What?" Dean was getting confused. Had Finneus thought him capable of stealing the Blood of Poseidon right out from under the queen's nose? "No, I have to go back. That was the plan."

"What are you talking about?" Finneus snapped. "You can't go back!"

"I can. There's a way in . . . I can get back in."

Finneus's features tightened with frustration. "You're not making any sense." He shook Dean hard. "Snap out of it! Is she dead or not?"

"What? Who?"

"The queen! Who else?"

"Why would she be . . . What are you talking about?"

"What are *you* talking about?" Finneus shot back. "What did you think I sent you in there to do?"

"I went in there to case the place. So later I could steal the Blood of Poseidon for Gentleman Jim. What did you want me to . . ."

Dean grasped the situation at last. If his thoughts hadn't been so jumbled by his metamorphosis, he might have realized what Finneus was saying sooner. "You wanted me to kill the queen?" Lyndra was right. Dean *was* part of a plot against the queen. He just hadn't known it!

"This is a fine mess," Finneus said, his voice bitter. Before Dean had a chance to swim away, Finneus grabbed his right arm and bent it painfully behind his back. Dean cried out as Finneus slipped a rope around his wrist and quickly went to work on the other arm.

"What are you doing?" Dean demanded.

"That should be obvious," Finneus told Dean for the second time in as many days. This time, there was no mistaking his intentions. Within seconds, he had Dean's upper body bound tightly with both hands pinned behind his back.

Fear jolted Dean's brain back to clarity. Finneus was going to kill him. It was the only way for him to clean up his "mess." Dean felt a tug as Finneus picked up the free end of the rope and swam off with him in tow. Their destination soon became clear. Vibrations in the water carried voices to Dean's ears. Instinctively, he made a noise of his own. It sped out in their direction and bounced back, allowing him to gauge the distance to whomever was out there. It turned out to be a whole throng of people.

Dean looked toward the source of the sound. It was dark and the group was far away, but Dean could see them just fine. He was adjusting to his new form more and more with each passing second. Dean's new eyes could see clear across the ocean floor. A large crowd had gathered at a deep underwater trench, with at least a thousand mermen and mermaids lined up on either side of the gorge. They floated in place, elbow to elbow, waiting for something . . . or someone. Dean's mouth fell open. It was Lightning Canyon. They were waiting for him.

He kicked and screamed. "Let me go!"

"Don't worry," Finneus said. "I will."

"You can't!" Dean pleaded. "You can't throw me in there like this!"

"Of course I can. You're a world-class daredevil."

Dean cursed and strained against the ropes, fighting to break free. It was no use. "Coward! You won't get away with this!"

"Get away with what?" Finneus waved to the crowd as they arrived at the canyon. The spectators cheered. "It's all part of the show."

CHAPTER 22

RIDE THE LIGHTNING

Finneus swooped over the mouth of the canyon and spun Dean around, tied up for all to see. He encouraged the crowd to give Dean a round of applause, and it responded with vigor. Dean tried to break free of his restraints. The audience simply assumed his struggling was part of the act, Dean showing off how tightly he'd been bound, and marveled at his bravery.

"Listen to that," Finneus told Dean. "You're a star."

Before Dean could call for help, Finneus pushed him backward into the canyon, giving Dean a mock salute as he fell. The last thing Dean saw as he drifted into the abyss was Ronan and Waverly. Their faces were pressed up against the glass window of their underwater pod-ship, high up above him in the crowd. They could tell something was wrong, but they were powerless to do anything about it. Dean was on his own. Just him and the eels.

He drifted down to the bottom, still struggling to get free. It was no use. He touched down gently, kicking up a cloud of soft, muddy silt on the canyon floor. His human ears would have considered this a silent landing, but his new mer-senses told him the reverberations would be enough to wake every eel in the canyon. He swam upright and braced himself for their arrival.

They didn't come right away.

As he waited, his skin felt the bite of freezing water. Dean couldn't tell if it was the icy temperature outside the city or the chill running down his spine that made him shiver. If he died down here, no one would ever know what Finneus had done. It would just look like he had bitten off more than he could chew— and the eels had taken the rest.

Dean twisted his body, squirming to loosen the ropes as he studied his surroundings. Even with his enhanced vision, it was hard to make anything out in water this dark. Lightning Canyon was long, deep, and crooked. Wide in some places and narrow in others, the shadowy gorge zigzagged back and forth for a good five hundred feet. Viewed from up above, the chasm had resembled the electric bolts of its namesake. Down below, the resemblance disappeared. Dean couldn't see past the winding canyon's first turn.

Eyes lit up in the darkness before him, one after another.

Dean spotted a pair here, a pair there . . . He counted at least five eels, all around him. Their eyes left eerie light trails in the black water. Dean had a feeling they saw him far better than he could see them.

Someone swam overhead, emptying a sack of glowing crystal pebbles as they passed. A storm of luminous gravel rained down into the canyon, lighting the stage. *It's not a show if the people can't see it*, Dean thought.

He shook off the pebbles, thankful to get a better look at what he was up against. Cave-sized holes pitted the walls of the trench. Dean watched as giant eel heads peeked out of their hiding spots, one after the other. Their gargantuan, snakelike frames were monstrous.

Dean was thankful Finneus hadn't bound his legs. He backed away from the eels as they moved in to get a closer look at him. He got a better look at them too, although he wished he hadn't. They were downright ghoulish with their green skin, opalescent blue eyes, and nostrils that extended out from their faces in tube-like growths. The eels opened their mouths wide, revealing jagged rows of thin, sharp teeth scattered across their lips. Each one of them had the gap-toothed grin of a sea witch, and looked just as friendly.

The eels started out fighting among themselves over who would get to eat Dean. As they snapped at each other, he kept trying to get loose, but the ropes remained tight as ever. Eventually, the largest of the eels asserted its dominance over the others and the infighting stopped. The alpha eel struck at Dean, and he barely dodged its attack.

The people watching above applauded, but Dean had no time to enjoy the crowd's adoration. Another eel snapped at him. Dean twisted his body in time to avoid its jaws, but the first eel swerved back for a second bite. A third eel zoomed past Dean, spinning him around. A shock rattled his bones as it grazed his skin. Dean realized the canyon's eels were charged with the same electric energy that split the sky during storms. The group of eels circled him, poised to strike again. He had to get away, but there was nowhere to go. *Swim!* he told himself. *Don't think, just swim!*

As another eel darted at him, Dean made a beeline for one of the empty holes in the canyon walls. At least, he hoped it was empty. Unable to fight, all Dean could do was flee. He entered the tunnel and swam until he hit a dead end. As he turned to look behind him, the alpha eel was right there. It gnashed its terrible teeth a few short feet away, but Dean was just out of reach.

The eels might have lived inside the tunnels, but they must have hunted by backing in tail-first and then springing out to chomp at their prey as it swam by. The eels couldn't seem to reach all the way to the rear of the tunnels when they went in headfirst.

Of course, that only earned Dean a brief respite from his ordeal—a moment to think, not an escape. What was he going to do?

He rubbed against the tunnel walls, trying to fray the ropes, but the walls were too smooth to cut them away. He wiggled and writhed until he managed to poke a hand out—the best he could do. Not enough to get free, but it was something. To escape, Dean needed help, and unfortunately, any help he got could only come from one place. He looked into the eyes of the giant chomping eel. It was still lodged in the tunnel, still relentless in its pursuit.

"I must be crazy."

Staying close to the wall, Dean backed down the tunnel, toward the frenzied eel. He had to time this just right. The eel's jaws came crashing down as expected, and Dean kicked off from the wall as hard as he could, sending himself flying toward the creature. He slammed into the eel's closed mouth and used his good hand to grab hold of the creature's long, disgusting nostril. The eel screeched and tried to snap at him, but Dean had flipped upside down, digging his heels in just under the eel's right eye. Try as it might, the eel could not bite its own nose.

Dean wasn't sure how long he could hold on, so he kicked the eel in the eye. It pulled out of the tunnel, recoiling like a snapped line and taking Dean with it. He went flying out of the hole like a cannonball. The crowd roared with delight to see him alive and unharmed, then groaned when he hit the canyon wall. Dean let out a groan of his own.

"Ow . . ."

As he fell back from the wall, Dean had no time to lick his wounds. The other eels were already coming for him. He steadied himself for their next assault. This time, he had something different in mind. He had to move, but not until he let one of the eels get in close enough.

The first eel dove at Dean. He inched back from its monstrous jaws at the last second, but the twisting leviathan rammed into him and sent him twirling around in the water. He went round and round, but when he stopped, the ropes fell away. The crowd erupted with cheers. Dean had used the eel's teeth to cut the rope. At last, he was on an equal footing with his attackers.

With his arms free, Dean was graceful and quick in the water, able to match the speed of the eels. They came at him all at once, but he swam circles around them, leading them on a merry ride. He went over, around, under, and through narrow gaps between the eels until three of them had tied themselves together in a knot. The bound eels shrieked and crackled. The crowd up above showered Dean with praise, loving every minute of his performance.

Dean couldn't deny feeling a rush himself, but he didn't want to push his luck. He had given the locals enough of a show. Far more than he had intended, in fact. It was time to make his exit. He looked to the end of the canyon. A long way down into shadows and darkness, he saw more glowing blue eyes blink open. There were too many of them. Breaking free of his restraints wasn't going to be enough. If he wanted to survive, he needed something more. *Think, Seaborne! How did you survive last time you got thrown in the water with a sea serpent?*

Dean snatched the length of rope he had been tied up with. It was just long enough for what he had in mind. He swam deeper into the canyon, and two eels behind him gave chase. Up ahead, more waited. The larger of the two eels behind him—the alpha—shoved the other one aside and caught up to Dean, trying to sink its teeth into him. Dean flipped up out of the way, and as the twisting monster flew by underneath him, he let out the rope, dropping it down before the creature's gaping maw. He slid it past the teeth until it reached the corners of the eel's mouth. Dean planted his feet on the back of the eel's neck and pulled back, holding the rope like the reins of a horse.

"Here we go, now! Yah!"

The big eel tried to throw him off, but Dean had done this kind of thing before and with a more tenuous grip. This time around, he had leverage on the eel and was actually able to steer it. Together, they plowed into the mass of other eels, scattering them. Dean directed the alpha to swerve from side to side, clearing the path and pushing its brethren out of the way. They lit up with shocks as Dean went by, but they could do nothing. He was rocketing through the canyon untouched on the back of the biggest, baddest eel in the ocean.

Despite the danger, Dean couldn't deny that it was an insane thrill. *Waverly must be rubbing off on me*, he thought.

Though the rest of the pack couldn't catch him, as Dean closed in on the other end of the canyon, the giant eel beneath him found a way to fight back. Why it waited so long to activate its electric current, Dean couldn't say. Perhaps it had been too angry to think straight earlier. Or perhaps eels just weren't the smartest of creatures. All Dean knew was that when the electricity traveled into his body, it was like no pain he had ever felt.

His blood might as well have been on fire, with his heart pumping the flames through his body, beating faster and faster. Dean didn't know if his heart was going to shut down or burst out the front of his chest, but they reached the end of the canyon, and the eel stopped short. For whatever reason, it would not leave its home, and that fact saved Dean's life—the sudden stop threw him over the eel's head and out into the open water.

He drifted, limp and weightless, as the crowd gave him a standing ovation. He had made it across Lightning Canyon. He was a star, just like Finneus had said. A falling star. He was tired. So tired . . . and everything hurt. Darkness crept around the corners of his vision. A golden figure swam out to catch him as the world around him faded into nothingness.

CHAPTER 23

CHANGE OF PLANS

Dean woke up in bed. He was lying on his belly, with his face tucked into a special circular pillow with a hole in the center like a nest. He was locked in position, unable to see anything but the floor below him.

Wherever Dean was, he was happy to be lying down. It was peaceful and quiet, the lighting was low, and he was out of the water—presumably, far away from Lightning Canyon. That was good. He never wanted to see another eel as long as he lived. Dean's entire body ached from being electrocuted. His skin felt like he'd been fried up in a sizzling pan, and his back twitched in pain every time he breathed in.

Someone pushed down hard along Dean's spine until he

heard a loud cracking noise, like a tree branch breaking. He didn't know what had just happened, but the pain in his back suddenly lessened. He tried to turn around and see who had done him such a wonderful service, but whoever it was pushed his head back down into the pillow.

"Don't move," he heard a woman whisper.

"Wherrrremmmm I?"

"Shhhh," the woman said. "Don't try to talk."

"You're safe," said another woman. "You were brought back to the city so we could treat your wounds."

Dean grunted. "Whooooorrrrrrryu?"

"The queen's royal healers," said the first woman, massaging his back. "Don't worry. We're going to take good care of you."

Dean nodded, already falling back asleep, safe in the knowledge that he was under the healers' care. The next few minutes passed for him in jerky time-jumps as he faded in and out of consciousness. His back felt better, but everything else still hurt.

One of the healers built a low fire on the floor beneath his face, then set a bowl of hot water atop it. Ingredients came next: fragrant herbs, crushed crystals, fine powders, drops of oil. The mixture turned blue-green and white vapors rose off it.

"Breathe," one of the healers said. Unable to do anything else, Dean took in the sweet-smelling infusion. The pain in his body faded more and more with each gulp of air. He felt himself breathing out toxins and getting stronger. His senses soon dulled.

Dean knew he was lying facedown on the bed, but he felt as though he was floating a foot in the air above it.

"You were wise to seek the sea god's blessing before entering the canyon," one of the healers told Dean. "Had your human frame taken such a shock from the eels, we might not have been able to revive you."

"Mer-people are slightly more resistant to electricity," the other healer said.

"Slightly," the first healer stressed.

They added fresh ingredients to the mixture Dean was breathing in. The aroma changed instantly, along with the sensation within Dean. Now, every time he drew in a breath, he felt his body being lowered back down onto the bed, inch by inch. The fog in his head lifted, and more importantly, his pain was gone. He felt awake and alive.

Dean propped himself up on his elbows. "What washh that?" he asked the healers, still slurring his words. "Whaddid you do?

The healers, who he was now seeing for the first time, were two matronly women with blue skin, black hair, and soft, easy smiles. "We did our job," the first one said. "Nothing more."

Dean slipped trying to sit up. He was still weak. The healers smiled and helped Dean turn around to lie on his back. "Don't push yourself." One of them propped him up with a pillow. "You need rest."

Once he was lying down facing the other way, Dean was

surprised to see Duke Shellheart standing at the foot of his bed. The duke looked as cheerful as ever.

"This young man has been through a lot," one of the healers told the duke. "If he's going to make a full recovery, he needs his sleep."

"We won't be long," Duke Shellheart replied.

The healers nodded and took their leave. After they left, the duke looked Dean up and down. "You made it. I'm impressed."

"You brought me here?" Dean guessed.

Shellheart nodded. "We needed to be here when you woke up. *If* you woke up."

Dean squinted at the duke. "We?"

The duke stepped aside to reveal Finneus seated in a chair directly behind him. The sight of the duplicitous young lord made Dean's blood run cold.

"You must have a thousand questions," Finneus said with a smile. "Ask away."

At first, Dean couldn't speak. He was too busy wondering how to get out of the healer's room alive. Shellheart stood blocking the only exit and Dean was in no condition to push past him. He could barely sit up, let alone stand and fight. If Finneus intended to finish what the eels had started, he was as good as dead.

"What's the point?" Dean managed to say at last. "You're here to kill me, aren't you?"

"That all depends," Finneus replied. "I have a few questions of my own first, starting with a man you obviously never met. Galen

Fishback. A month ago, I sent him to the surface to hire humans with a very specific set of skills. Tell me, how is it that you came to replace them?"

Increasingly, Dean understood the situation he and his friends had wandered into. The men on the ship that Skinner had raided, the ones he had forced to walk the plank . . . they weren't entertainers hired to perform for the queen after all. They had been cutthroats hired to kill her. That was who Finneus had thought Dean, Ronan, and Waverly were when they arrived. Lyndra too.

"It's a long story," Dean said. "Your assassins ran into a bit of trouble on the way here."

"Where are they now?"

Dean shook his head. "They're not coming."

"What are you doing here?" asked Shellheart. "Why did you come to Atlantis?"

"That much I know already," Finneus said. "He's here for his friend Harper. The one in prison." He leaned forward in his chair toward Dean. "What I don't know is why you thought I'd want to help you break him out of jail."

Dean sighed, wondering how he could have misread the situation so badly. "Last night, you said he could leave with us. This city runs on tourism. Killer humans are bad for business. Those were your exact words."

Finneus sat up in his chair. "That's what you thought we were talking about? Saving my aunt's blasted human circus?" The young lord pressed a palm against his forehead. "I thought *you and your friend* were my killer humans." He looked up at Shellheart. "I keep trusting the wrong people. It's Fishback all over again."

"Fishback," Dean said, realizing the truth. "You killed him, not Gentleman Jim."

"Actually, I killed him," Shellheart said with a grotesque air of pride. "Lord Finneus needed my help and I was happy to oblige."

Finneus shrugged his shoulders, as if some things just couldn't be helped. "Fishback left us no choice. He was going to tell Captain Lyndra everything. I couldn't have that. The idea was to pin his death on her, but your friend Harper ruined that by confessing to his murder." Finneus cast his eyes upward. "Don't ask me why. I told you, his mind's not right. Even so, despite the trouble he caused, I was prepared to let you leave here with him, but only after you did what was necessary to put me on the throne."

"What was *necessary*?" Dean asked, disgusted. "You wanted me to kill your aunt just so you could be king sooner rather than later. That's hardly necessary. And you," he added, looking at Shellheart. "What do you get out of this? Let me guess. War with Abyssal."

Shellheart smiled. "Don't mind if I do."

"It's going to happen eventually," Finneus said. "We might as well get on with it. And it's for the best, really. The Abyssians are *so* unpleasant."

Dean scowled at Finneus. "How can someone who lives on the ocean floor be this shallow?"

Finneus laughed. "That's good. You're very clever. Maybe clever enough to stay useful."

"Why are you telling me all this? If you want your crown and your war so badly, you could just take the queen out yourself. You obviously have no qualms about killing. You don't need me."

"Killing a craven turncoat like Fishback is one thing," Finneus replied. "Killing the queen of Atlantis is something else entirely. My aunt rules with the divine authority of Poseidon himself. No god-fearing merman would dare raise a hand against her."

"That's why you needed human assassins," Dean said. "Sorry. I told you, they're not coming. Ever."

"Fortunately for us, we still have you."

"I'm not a killer."

"I know. You're a thief. A sneak. Which means it's not too late to salvage a mutually beneficial relationship. You've proven yourself both resourceful and brave. But are you smart enough to make a bargain? Are you willing to do what's necessary to save yourself and your friends?"

Dean stared at Finneus and Shellheart for a long moment. As much as he despised the two of them, he had no choice but to hear them out. "I'm listening."

"It's simple. You were going to steal the Blood of Poseidon for your friend Gentleman Jim. Steal it for me instead. If you can do that, no one has to die. Not even the queen. Surely, she told you what the blood does . . ."

"She did."

"Once I drink it, I'll be the one infused with the sea god's power. I'll be the one they fear."

At that, Dean could only fold his arms.

"Can you find your way back into Poseidon's Chamber or can't you?" asked Duke Shellheart.

Dean pictured the chamber in his head. "I can get in."

"Good. This should be an easy decision for you," said Finneus.

"Helping you overthrow the queen? Starting a war?"

"What do you care about that?" Shellheart asked.

"Indeed," Finneus agreed. "Who's king, who's queen? Will it be war or peace? It doesn't concern you. Before yesterday, you didn't even know the Mer-Realm existed. After you and your friends leave Atlantis, your lives won't be affected by what goes on down here, one way or the other."

"Or none of you could leave Atlantis," Shellheart proposed. "Ever."

"Once again, my esteemed colleague speaks the truth," Finneus told Dean. "You can't afford to have us as enemies, Dean Seaborne. And you'll never leave this room if we can't be friends. You know too much. But you have a chance to live through this and save the lives of your friends in the bargain. One answer, right now. Are you in or out?"

Dean gritted his teeth. "In. But it has to be tonight."

CHAPTER 24

FIGHT NIGHT

That evening, it was Ronan's turn to join the human circus. Night had fallen, and once again, half the city had gathered outside the palace. Following Dean's performance with the eels that afternoon, the people of Atlantis couldn't wait to see what he and his friends would do next.

"Another sellout crowd," Finneus had told Dean before leaving to oversee the evening's festivities. "We couldn't have asked for a better diversion." Atlanteans and tourists had begun filling into the plaza early, and now, with only moments left before showtime, the excitement in the air was palpable.

An eight-sided cage had been built in the center of the plaza. Inside it, two champions, one from Abyssal and the other from

Neptune, were sparring with each other and warming up the crowd. They were the undercard. Ronan's fight was to be the main event. A bare-knuckle brawl between him and a famous fighter from Atlantis. Dean watched the action unfold from the edge of the plaza, with Shellheart serving as his escort. The duke had been with Dean ever since they had left the healer's room. Shellheart and Finneus weren't taking any chances with him. Not when they were so close to achieving their goal.

Dean looked on longingly as Waverly taped up Ronan's hands before the big fight. As far as Dean's friends knew, he was still in the healer's room, his life hanging by a thread. There was some truth to that idea. If Dean stole the Blood of Poseidon, he would make a "miraculous recovery" and be released. If he failed, he would "succumb to his injuries" and never be heard from again. That was the deal—the only one on the table. Dean's lack of options didn't make him feel any better about helping Finneus and Shellheart with their plan.

"This will all be over soon enough," Shellheart told Dean. "Just do as you're told, and you'll get what you want." The duke smiled as the Neptunian fighter pounded away at his Abyssian opponent. "We all will."

"Be careful what you wish for," replied Dean.

"What was that?"

Dean shrugged. "I'm just saying . . . wishes have a way of not working out, even after they come true. Take it from me, I've been doing other people's dirty work my whole life. I thought I had put all that behind me, but I was wrong. I'm not free. Maybe I never was."

"Am I supposed to feel sorry for you?"

"You just better be sure this is what you want, is all." Dean nodded to the ring. The Abyssian fighter rallied and went to work on the man from Neptune. "I know I wouldn't pick a fight with these guys."

Suddenly, the bulky, gray-skinned Abyssian had the pale, limber fighter from Neptune on the ropes. He landed blow after blow to the smaller man's head as the crowd cheered for a knockout. Shellheart frowned as the Abyssian fighter crouched low to duck a flailing punch and then sprang up with a devastating uppercut. The force of the blow lifted Neptune's champion into the air. He landed hard on the mat, and the crowd erupted with a roar so loud Dean had to cover his ears. The noise level was particularly impressive given the silence of anyone who hailed from Neptune.

Shellheart made a face like he was chewing on a clove of garlic. "The real fight will be much, much different."

"But hasn't the fighting been over for a hundred years? Your people can't *all* want war . . ."

The duke scoffed. "Don't presume to tell me what my men want. We would have had war long ago if not for the queen. That will change. You'll see. This city isn't a melting pot. It's a powder keg."

Finneus entered the ring and raised the Abyssian fighter's arm in the air, officially declaring him the winner. "A triumphant performance!" he said, congratulating the combatant on his victory. "Ladies and gentlemen, I give you the new heavyweight champion of the sea!" Half the crowd went wild. Shellheart balled a fist. Scores of his pale-skinned countrymen shouted out boos and worse.

"And now, for something entirely different . . ." Finneus motioned for Ronan to join him in the ring. "In this corner, I give you a young man from the surface with a strength and courage that belies his age. Put your hands together for Ronan MacGuire!"

The crowd showered Ronan with praise.

"It's time," Shellheart said, handing Dean a satchel. "Here. The tools you requested."

Dean took the bag and slung it over his shoulder. "Just a minute. I want to see who Ronan's fighting first."

"If I were you, I'd worry about my own self," Shellheart warned him. "If you fail tonight, or try to betray us in any way, you won't live long enough to regret it. Your friends down there will share your fate. I'll see to that personally."

"You people," Dean said, "you're all the same. Always threatening, even after I've agreed to do what you want. I just want to see what my friend's up against."

Ronan climbed into the ring to the sound of thunderous applause. He bounced around on the balls of his feet, throwing jabs, oblivious to the acclaim. Finneus directed the crowd's attention to the south side of the plaza, where two footmen were wheeling in a rusty metal box the size of a coffin. "And, in this corner . . . a creature that requires no introduction. Beware . . . the Sponge!"

Dean's face contorted. "The Sponge? What kind of a nickname is that for a fighter?"

The duke smirked. "It's no nickname."

Dean stared at the curiosity being wheeled in to fight Ronan. Heavy chains had been wrapped around the metal box, and there was a small window with iron bars on the front. Something behind the bars was banging on the door, trying to get out.

Ronan stopped moving. He looked rattled as the men propped the box up against an opening in the cage, directly across from him. Finneus hustled out of the ring as they loosed the chains. The thing inside pounded once . . . twice . . . On the third time, the door flew off its hinges and a freakish behemoth squeezed its way out. The crowd was simultaneously revolted and thrilled. The sight transfixed Dean. He didn't know what to call the beast that emerged from the box. It had the shape of a man, but *monster* was the only word for it.

The creature was eight feet tall if it was a foot and covered head to toe with a layer of heavy, sopping sea sponges. Unless the thing was made of sea sponge all the way through. The sponges seemed to come together on its face in the shape of two eyes and a nose. As its mouth opened up, the creature bellowed with a bone-chilling, mindless moan. The Sponge began lumbering toward Ronan, leaving briny, wet footprints on the mat as it stumbled forth.

"Now you know what he's up against," said the duke. "I could have told you that knowledge would do nothing to boost your spirits." He eased Dean away from the plaza. "Off you go now, little merman. You have a job of your own."

Dean took a tortured last look over his shoulder as the duke guided him away. Ronan looked like he wanted to run from the Sponge, but there was nowhere to hide inside the ring. There was nothing Dean could do to help him, either. Nothing beyond what he was already doing, that is. He had to leave, and if he didn't come back with the Blood of Poseidon, Ronan would have faced that monster for nothing. Dean just hoped his friends—all his friends—would survive whatever happened next.

CHAPTER 25

THE HEIST

Dean hurried out to the city limits. His destination was the same place where Lyndra had questioned him and his mates so harshly upon their arrival. The spot was out of the way, sandwiched between two buildings, and as dark an alley as one could hope to find in Atlantis. Dean wagered that hardly anyone went down there on a normal day, and with the world's strangest boxing match in full swing, the alley would be more deserted than usual.

Alone in the alley, Dean stepped to the edge of Atlantis, where the Heavy Water barrier cut a line between air and ocean. It was like standing beside a waterfall. Thousands of gallons of Heavy Water rained down from above. The substance didn't hit the ocean floor, as Dean had originally assumed, but instead disappeared into a trench that had been cut around the city. Looking at the Atlantean border now, it was a wonder how he ever could have missed the trench. A metal grate with iron bars covered the chasm surrounding Atlantis. The bars were set too close together for a person to slip between. But if they weren't there . . .

Dean opened the satchel of tools that Shellheart had given him. He didn't need much. The bag included a strong rope with a claw hook and a small glass vial with a cork top. He set those aside and removed the last two items out of the satchel, a pry bar and mallet. Dean took one last look around as he tossed the empty bag aside. "No sense waiting any longer."

Dean went to work, sliding the pry bar under a section of grating. Next, he pushed down as hard as he could, forcing the grate up. Unfortunately, that was all he could do. The weight of the water pounding against the grate was too much. Dean couldn't move it.

He took his rope and tied it through the bars. Putting all his weight on the pry bar, he pulled again. And once again, he failed to draw it out. The iron bars were too heavy and the water was too strong. But Dean had come too far to give up now.

One of the buildings in the alley had a row of columns across its exterior. Dean threw the end of his rope around one of them. Stepping down on the pry bar and pulling the rope around the column like a pulley, he gave it one last go. The rope began to fray as he pulled it, but the added leverage allowed him to tow the grate out of its position. Having opened the door to Poseidon's Chamber, Dean fell to his knees, exhausted. "Get up," he told himself. "You're just getting started."

Dean gathered up his rope, tucked the vial into his pocket, and sat down next to the downpour of Heavy Water. He took a breath, said a little prayer, and pushed himself into the chasm.

He went down like an anchor chain. The Heavy Water beat against him like a thousand hammers, but he weathered the storm as he traveled beneath the city, completely submerged. Dean never would have attempted the drop in a human body. Not because he would have drowned—he wouldn't have lived long enough to drown. The raging current would have flipped him around until it broke his neck. But as a merman, he went with the flow.

The water fired him farther down, until he descended into darkness. But just as before, he could still see so much. No matter how little light was there, his heightened sight let him take in his surroundings. It took less than a minute for the furious water to reach Poseidon's Chamber. Having been there before, Dean knew exactly what he was looking for, and he was ready. As the water entered the chamber, he went flying into the air and threw out the hook.

It latched onto the platform below the water tank, and Dean hung on tight, swinging out and back again. Eventually, the rope steadied, and Dean dangled there with Heavy Water pouring down on all sides. Below him, the massive wheels that powered the water filter spun wildly. On the platform above him, he saw the statue of Poseidon, unguarded. "No one here," Dean smiled. He started climbing up, hand over hand. "Too easy."

No sooner had he said that than the frayed rope began to unravel. It didn't snap, holding Dean's weight, but there was no telling how much longer it would do so.

"Blast it!" Dean cursed. What now? Should he go slower or try to climb faster and get up past the unraveling section of rope before it broke? If he chose wrong, he'd be shot out into the sea empty-handed and his friends would be doomed.

Dean opted to go slow. He pulled once on the rope and watched another thread pop. He froze, afraid to move another inch. He couldn't get up that way. He'd never make it. But what could he do?

He looked around the cavern. *Think, Seaborne! Everyone's counting on you.* His eyes swept the walls. There was nothing there to help him, unless . . . *That's it! The walls!*

Unable to climb up, and with no reason to climb down, Dean decided to try another direction. He moved his legs back and forth, building up momentum and swinging the rope from side to side. It started small at first, but he was soon traveling across the cavern in a wide arc. The movement was also taxing on the rope, but this way, when the rope finally gave out, Dean would still have a chance. He flew across the chamber like the pendulum of a grandfather clock until forward momentum carried him all the way to the wall. He latched on to one of the pipes fixed on the sides of the chamber and held on for dear life.

From there, Dean climbed, looking more like a monkey-man than a merman, until he was directly over the platform housing Poseidon. Dean let go, dropping twenty feet and landing hard on his side. It hurt like the devil, but the pain came with purpose, and it put a smile on his face. He had reached the statue. Dean staggered to his feet and checked the glass vial in his pocket. Thankfully, it had not shattered.

"Too easy," he whimpered, but he wasn't being entirely ironic. As he emptied the goblet of Poseidon's blood into the vial, Dean had to admit this step could have been much harder. If any guards had been posted here, he wouldn't have stood a chance.

He corked the vial after filling it to the brim and then gathered up the top half of his rope, which was still hooked onto the metal platform. He was about to throw the rope into the water below when a troubling realization hit him:

It didn't matter if he delivered the blood or not. Finneus and Shellheart were going to kill him either way. That had been Finneus's plan from the start. Dean's fist tightened around the rope. "That slippery eel."

Dean stowed the vial and leaped into the water.

He passed under the water filter and out into the sea, just as he had done earlier that morning. This time, he was not the least bit disoriented when the ride deposited him in a cold stretch of ocean, leagues away from Atlantis. He wasn't the least bit surprised to find Finneus and Shellheart there waiting for him, either.

"Is the fight over already?" Dean asked.

"I left early," Finneus replied. "Your friend was losing. It was hard to watch."

Dean gritted his teeth.

"Did you get it?" Shellheart asked.

Moving slowly and deliberately, Dean produced the vial.

Finneus's eyes lit up. "You did! Give it to me!" He swam forward, his hands reaching out, but Dean backed up.

"Hold it right there." Dean pressed his thumb against the cork in the vial, applying just enough pressure to let a drop of the sacred blood escape.

Finneus stopped short. "Stop! What are you doing?"

Dean wagged a finger. "Not so fast, Finneus. You and I are going to have a little talk first."

CHAPTER 26

THE GREAT ESCAPE

"Stay back or I swear I'll empty every drop of this into the sea."

"You wouldn't dare," Shellheart growled.

"Try me."

Finneus froze. "Easy now, Seaborne. Don't do anything rash," he said, trying to turn the charm back on. "We're all in this together. Think of your friends."

"I am," said Dean. "I'm wondering how you plan to kill them after you're through with me. Quick and easy, or are you going to take your time and have some fun with it?"

"What?" Finneus was all smiles. "No! Why would I want to . . . ?" His voice cracked mid-sentence. "I don't want to kill anyone."

"Maybe you think I forgot about the last time we were here. After you sent me to kill the queen? You tied me up and threw me to the eels."

"That was so you wouldn't talk! I made a mistake. It's different now."

"Because of this," Dean said, brandishing the vial. "But tell me something." Dean held up the rope that he had used to break into Poseidon's Chamber. "The rope you used to tie me up this morning. Why did you have it with you to begin with?"

Finneus's smile faded. "What?"

"The truth is, you were planning to kill me even if I *had* assassinated the queen," Dean said. "Don't bother denying it."

Finneus sighed. "I did say you were clever. What do you want?"

"For starters, I want you to honor our deal. I want out of here. Safe passage to the surface for me and my friends. I also want the gold that Queen Avenel promised us. Otherwise . . ." He grabbed the cork, ready to take the top off and spill out the contents of the vial.

Shellheart drew his sword. "You open that vial and I'll run you through without a second thought."

"If I hand it over, you'll do the same thing. Seems to me I might as well."

"No!" cried Finneus. He paused and tried to regain his composure. "Enough. You win. Just . . . don't do anything we'll all regret."

"A bit late for that, don't you think?" someone asked.

A black blur streaked through the water toward Dean. Whatever it was grabbed the hook end of Dean's rope and pulled him away. The violent jerk nearly caused him to lose control of the vial containing the Blood of Poseidon. He tucked it away and held on tight to the rope line. Dean's first thought was that Finneus or Shellheart had managed to hit him with a sneak attack, but he was moving away from them at a high speed. Dean turned and was shocked to see who had grabbed hold of him.

"Captain Lyndra?"

She reached for Dean's hand and pulled him atop the back of a black manta. "Hang on. You're coming with me."

Once Dean was firmly on board the fish, he looked behind him and saw Finneus and Shellheart shrink from sight. "Where did you come from?" he asked Lyndra.

She kept her eyes fixed forward, racing back to Atlantis. "Abyssal, originally."

Dean blinked. *Did she just make a joke?* "How did you know I'd be here? Were you following me?"

"I've been following you since you got here. After you went through the grate at the edge of the city, I knew there was only one place for you to come out."

She took a hard turn to starboard, banking toward a gap in the Magic Mountains. Dean held onto the manta for dear life. He couldn't believe his luck. She was just the person he needed to tell about Finneus and Shellheart. "Lyndra, the plot against the queen. You were right!"

"Of course I was right. My only mistake was that I thought you were working with either Finneus *or* Shellheart. I should have known it was the two of them together."

"Working with them?" Dean said. "You don't understand, they forced me to—"

"Don't try to worm your way out of this. I heard you talking. You said he sent you to kill the queen."

"That was a mix-up. I didn't know he wanted me to kill her."

Lyndra's eyes narrowed. She didn't believe Dean for a second. From her point of view, she hadn't rescued him. She had captured him. The water around them grew brighter as they approached the glowing mountain range outside the city. "Where are you taking me?"

Lyndra scoffed. "Where do you think? I'm bringing you before the queen. I'm going to tell her everything, and this time she's going to listen. Thanks to you, I finally have the full story."

"I have to see my friends first," Dean said. "They're in danger."

"You're in no position to ask me for anything."

"Please," Dean pleaded.

"Be quiet!" Lyndra ordered. "You're not talking your way out of this. Not after what you've done."

Dean held his tongue, silently cursing himself and his predicament. Lyndra could have been a valuable ally, but it was too late for that. She'd never trust a word he said. Dean didn't exactly blame her, but he couldn't let her take him in, either. He scanned the ocean as they flew along on the giant manta's back. They reached a path that ran between the Magic Mountains, and Dean had to shield his eyes from the glare. Hoping that the light had temporarily blinded Lyndra as well, he acted fast, throwing his rope's grappling hook off the manta and tying a quick knot with the rope's free end.

"What are you doing?" Lyndra asked as the hook dug into the crystal terrain below them. A second later, the rope yanked her off the speeding manta by the wrist.

"Sorry, I've got places to be that don't include jail," Dean said, sliding over to take control of the fish. "At least, not in a cell of my own." The manta bucked, sensing Dean's inexperience, but he held on long enough to figure out how to steer the creature through the mountain path alone.

He reached Atlantis and found the spot where Gentleman Jim was being held. Just as Dean remembered, there were no guards on the water side of Jim's cell. He checked behind him and was grateful to find that neither Lyndra nor Finneus and Shellheart had caught up with him yet. Dean ditched the manta and swam up to the Heavy Water barrier, hugging the ground as he went. The idea was to get Gentleman Jim out of the city first and then go back for Ronan and Waverly. He didn't have a plan past that point, but so far, all his plans had gone sideways in a hurry. He doubted he could do any worse making things up as he went along.

Dean dove through the Heavy Water barrier, landing right inside Gentleman Jim's cell. Gentleman Jim jumped out of bed, startled by Dean's sudden appearance. "You! What are you doing here?"

"What does it look like?" Dean asked. "I'm here to rescue you."

"What?"

"I'm breaking you out."

Gentleman Jim turned around to look at the front door of his cell. "How?"

Dean shook his head. "Not that way."

"What other way is there to . . ." Gentleman Jim trailed off, perhaps realizing that Dean was—for the time being—a merman. "You look different."

"Just give me your hand. There's no time to explain."

"I thought I told you to go home. Forget about me."

"You also told me no one gets left behind."

"I never said that."

"How would you know? You don't even remember meeting me."

Gentleman Jim made a face that said he couldn't argue. "I'll fill you in later," Dean continued. "For now, just brace yourself. This is going to feel a little weird." He took out the vial of the Blood of Poseidon. "Well, if you want the truth, it's going to hurt like the devil."

"What is that?" Gentleman Jim asked as Dean took his hand.

Dean uncorked the vial and spilled out a drop onto Gentleman Jim's palm. "You'll see."

Dean squirmed uncomfortably as the blood transformed Gentleman Jim. The freezing cold, the blinding light, the excruciating pain in the chest . . . having been through it himself, the process was hard for Dean to watch. To his credit, Gentleman Jim didn't make a sound.

The "blessing of the sea god" concluded with Gentleman Jim stumbling around his cell, clawing at his throat in a desperate attempt to breathe. Dean remembered that feeling too.

"To the sea!" he said, pointing at the watery fourth wall of Gentleman Jim's cell. "Go!"

What once had been a prison wall was now an open door. Gentleman Jim dove through the waterfall barrier and out into the ocean. Dean followed him out. On the other side, Dean found him a few feet off, swimming in circles. Gentleman Jim had started testing out his new body and feeling around with his new senses. If he was anything like Dean, he would adjust quickly.

"It's all right," Dean said. "Just follow me and do as I do. We need to find the others before it's too late."

Unfortunately, it was already too late. Dean saw Gentleman Jim staring at something behind him: Captain Lyndra, who was floating a few feet off. Strangely, she made no move against them.

"You used the blood to set him free?" she said. Her voice was soft. Shocked. "That's why you wanted it?"

"That's why *I* wanted it," Dean replied and then pointed past Lyndra. "It's not why *they* wanted it."

"Stop!" cried Finneus, arriving at last alongside Duke Shellheart. They had commandeered a pair of sea horses and were riding in hard and fast.

"Guards!" shouted Shellheart. "Your prisoner is escaping!"

The guards on the dry side of the Heavy Water barrier looked up from their posts and shook with surprise. Wasting no time, they dove through the barrier and came surging through the water toward Dean and the fugitive Gentleman Jim. Lyndra looked back and forth between the guards and Gentleman Jim and then spoke the last words Dean expected to hear:

"Go."

Dean's eyes were the size of sand dollars. "Go? You were just—"

"Go now!" she yelled at Dean and Gentleman Jim, and swam off to intercept the guards. There were four of them and only one of her, but she went at them with the tenacity of a shark. Meanwhile, Shellheart and Finneus were closing in. Dean knew Gentleman Jim was in no condition for a fight. It would take at least a few minutes more before he acclimated to his new merform. They had to flee. Dean grabbed Gentleman Jim's wrist and pulled. "Come on!"

As they darted through the water, Dean frantically scanned the seascape for a cave opening or a reef. They needed a place to hide. What he saw instead was a winding trail of glowing water off in the distance. The Waterway!

Behind them, Shellheart and Finneus had gained ground quickly. Just before Dean and Gentleman Jim reached the current, Dean felt something grab his foot. He turned around to see Shellheart's snarling face. "Where do you think you're going?"

Riding to the rescue once again, Lyndra barreled into the duke, knocking him off his sea horse. Dean briefly pictured four guards unconscious in the water near Gentleman Jim's former cell. As Shellheart spun away, Finneus charged in with a knife. Lyndra caught him by the wrist and twisted his arm, pulling him off his mount as well.

Dean moved to drag Gentleman Jim away as Lyndra resumed grappling with Shellheart. "We have to get out of here!" Dean said. The Waterway was right there. Just a few more feet, and he and Jim would be gone.

Since becoming a merman, Dean had swum into hard current more than once. He had done it both times that he had exited Poseidon's Chamber, and also when he had snuck back in. But entering the Waterway would be different. The last time Dean took this ride, he had been strapped into a seat that had been bolted to the floor inside a strong metal sphere. He had been protected. He had planned to go home with the same protections in place, but circumstances dictated otherwise. Instead, he and Gentleman Jim charged into the Waterway headfirst, helpless against its fury.

Salt water pounded Dean's body as he coursed through the depths at a blistering pace. The current flipped him around, feeling more like mortar than water, with a force that would have broken an air-breather's neck. Dean went limp and tried not to fight it. He hoped Gentleman Jim realized the only way through this was to try and become one with the flow. Dean would see him on the other side—if they made it.

The sea grew bitterly cold, and then warm again, as Dean and Gentleman Jim passed through arctic waters on their way home. As they flew along, they were pelted by all manner of sand and shell. The tiny grains felt to Dean like a million pins, pricking his skin over and over. There was no way to avoid it. He couldn't have moved his arms to cover himself up if he tried. The only relief came whenever the Waterway current twisted him around so he faced away from the oncoming sediment, and then when the ride finally ended.

The Waterway spat out Dean and Gentleman Jim in almost exactly the same spot where Dean had first found it. They exited the current beneath the sea and drifted up, doing the dead man's float.

By the time Dean reached the surface, his rejuvenation at the hands of the Atlantean healers had been completely negated. He felt like he'd been beaten with a sack of rocks. He turned around slowly and tried to get his bearings. He spied Aquatica on the horizon in one direction and a ship anchored far off in the other—Skinner's ship, the *Crimson Tide*. Gentleman Jim came up for air next, coughing and spitting out salt water. Dean went to check on him.

"Are you all right?"

Gentleman Jim turned around, his eyes drifting as if he'd just been on the receiving end of a knockout punch. Then his entire body shook as Dean came into focus. "Seaborne?" he exclaimed. "Can that be you?" A moment later, he grabbed Dean by the shoulders, nearly pulling them both under. "It is! I don't believe it!"

Dean smiled. "Good to have you back, Cap'n."

Gentleman Jim looked around. "What about the others?" he asked. "Where's everybody else?"

PART FIVE

SINK OR SWIM

CHAPTER 27

BACK SO SOON?

"Was that Lyndra?" Gentleman Jim asked.

Dean nodded. Gentleman Jim appeared to be struggling with the flood of long-term and short-term memories that had just returned to him. He looked around for Captain Lyndra as if she were right nearby.

"She's not here, Cap'n," said Dean.

"What about Ronan and your friend, the girl? Surely they got out before you came for me."

"No." Dean shook his head. "We left them behind." He felt ill as the words left his mouth.

"Seaborne! I told you to leave *me* behind! What were you thinking?"

"This wasn't the plan."

"I should hope not! We need to go back. We've got to fix this!"

"Aye, sir. We've got our work cut out for us."

"First things first." Gentleman Jim scanned the horizon. "There's a ship there. If we're lucky, the people on board are friendly."

"We're not lucky. That's a pirate ship."

"You know it?"

"Too well. Nothing but murderous scoundrels on board—worst I've seen since One-Eyed Jack. He's dead, by the way."

Gentleman Jim's mouth fell open. "What?"

"You heard me. It's a whole new world up here, Cap'n. At least, it was supposed to be. I'll fill you in on the way. We need to make that ship before sunrise."

"You have a plan for dealing with its crew?" Gentleman Jim said.

Dean squinted at the *Crimson Tide*. "I might. Their captain ... he's an ice-blooded blackguard, but he knows the value of a good deal."

The ship was several leagues away. The swim would have been difficult, if not impossible, for anyone saddled with human legs (and lungs). But in their transformed state, it proved to be an easy task. They reached Skinner's ship in less than an hour.

Along the way, Dean took time to catch Gentleman Jim up on everything he had missed. First, he explained how they had survived the wreck of their ship, the *Reckless*. Then he told Jim what had become of One-Eyed Jack. That tale ended with Gentleman Jim's former crew, the Pirate Youth, alive and well, free to live out their days on the enchanted Golden Isle of Zenhala. Gentleman Jim was overjoyed to hear that part of the story, but it didn't change the fact that one member of his crew was still unaccounted for. As long as Ronan stayed in Atlantis, he was in more danger than ever—assuming he hadn't already been smothered by the Sponge. Waverly wasn't safe either. If Dean and Gentleman Jim hoped to have any chance of getting them back, they were going to need some help.

When they reached the *Crimson Tide*, they dove down deep beneath the ship and came up on the other side fast enough to fly out of the water. They shot up into the air like jumping porpoises and landed on the deck. Dean touched down right next to a half-asleep pirate who was attempting to stand watch.

"Gah!" the man exclaimed, nearly falling over. Gentleman Jim's sudden appearance had the same effect on Long Tom Cannon. He uttered a soft "Boo!" that sent the big man reeling. Long Tom backpedaled away, tripping over a few pirates who were sleeping on deck, and then fell on top of them. They cried out in discomfort, and it wasn't long before the whole ship was awake.

"What's going on here?" Marlon Spyke demanded, crossing the deck. "By the powers!" he said, stopping short to gawk at Dean and Gentleman Jim. Standing in the light of the moon, with their pale blue skin, the two of them looked like ghosts.

"Where's Skinner?" asked Dean.

"In his cabin," Spyke replied, his eyes the size of doubloons.

"Get him up."

Spyke nodded. "Long Tom . . . wake the captain. Seaborne's back."

Lanterns were lit as the crew waited for its captain to come out on deck. The pirates surrounded Dean and Gentleman Jim on all sides. Just like the last time Dean was on board Skinner's ship, he was hopelessly outnumbered. Unlike the last time, Dean was not at all afraid. Skinner was a heartless rogue, but he was also doggedly pragmatic. Right now, he knew nothing of what had transpired since Dean had last been in his sight. Dean held all the cards, and Skinner wouldn't touch him until he found out what they were.

"What's all this, then?" Skinner asked when at last he emerged from his cabin. "Seaborne, is that you? We wasn't expecting your signal 'til tomorrow morning."

"Things have changed."

Skinner took a lantern and held it up to get a good look at Dean. "I can see that," he said, noting his blue skin. "What's happened to you, lad?"

"It's been an interesting couple of days."

"Clearly." Skinner turned his attention to Gentleman Jim. "And who might you be, friend?"

Gentleman Jim puffed his chest. "Gentleman Jim Harper, formerly a captain in One-Eyed Jack's Black Fleet. And I'm not your friend. You have a prisoner. A man called Verrick. We want to see him."

Skinner scowled. "That sounded ta me like an order. I'm the only one giving orders on this ship." He pointed at Dean. "I ordered *you* to get me into Aquatica. I don't care if you come back here blue, green, or purple. It don't change anything. The only color that matters to me is gold."

"You're wrong, Skinner," Dean said. "Everything's changed. The good news is, I can get you into Aquatica. The bad news is, there's nothing there."

"What are you talking about?"

"Aquatica's a smokescreen. It's not a holiday spot for kings and queens. It's a border station. The gateway to Atlantis. If you want your treasure, you're going to have to go a little farther to get it."

Half the crew laughed their heads off at what Dean had told them. The other half laughed even harder.

"Listen ta that fish tale!"

"You expect us ta believe that?"

"What kind of fools do ya take us for?"

As the crew guffawed, showing off black-toothed smiles that had never once been brushed, Skinner stood in silence. He put a hand up, a signal to quiet the crew. The rowdy laughter ground to a halt.

"Ordinarily, I'd be suspicious of such a story," Skinner began. "But things being the way they are . . ." He motioned to Dean's strange appearance, then turned to his crew. "Get the prisoner."

Skinner's crew was so shocked to hear him say he believed Dean that none of them moved.

"You scalawags hard of hearing!?" Skinner bellowed. "Get the prisoner, I say!"

The crew scattered. Most of them did not come back, but they did push Verrick out from below deck. He climbed through a hatch, looking weary and beaten, but the sight of Dean breathed life into him.

"Dean!" Verrick said, stumbling forth. "What's happened to you? Where's Waverly?"

"She's fine," Dean said. "Last I saw her, anyway. She won't be for long, unless we go get her. In Atlantis."

"Atlantis!"

"Hold on a blasted minute," Skinner said. "You're not going anywhere. I need to think about this."

"What's there to think about?" Gentleman Jim asked Skinner. "You want your treasure, don't you?"

"That's right. You're not going to get any richer waiting around here," Dean said. "Go on, hoist that sail and set a course for Aquatica. We haven't any time to lose."

"How are we going to get in?" Skinner wanted to know. "Is your other friend in there, waiting to lower the gate?"

"No. He's in Atlantis too."

"I don't have another flag with me," Skinner said. "And if memory serves, before you ran up the one I gave you, they nearly blew you out of the water."

"I've nothing to gain from getting your ship fired upon. Not as long as I'm a passenger on board."

"So how do we get in without the flag?"

"Leave that to me," Dean said. "I've got something better than a flag."

"Really? What?"

"That's my business."

Skinner stroked the stubble on his cheeks. "You're a cagey one, Seaborne. Just remember, so am I. We'll make for Aquatica, but all the way there, you'll stand where I can see you with a sword at your back. If this is a trick . . . if we walk into an ambush, or they fire so much as one shot at us—even by accident—you'll be dead before the cannonball leaves the cannon."

"I'm not worried," Dean said, putting on a brave front.

Skinner barked orders at his men, and the *Crimson Tide* set sail for Aquatica. The sun was not yet up, and the fortress at sea loomed large in the fading moonlight. Dean, standing at the bow of the ship, advised a direct approach to avoid the mines that surrounded Aquatica.

The sun was rising as they closed in on the main gate. Dean quietly hoped that Mookergwog's watch would be less vigilant this time around, but a pirate stationed up in the crow's nest called out movement on the castle walls. Dean saw it too. A cannon behind the battlements had pointed its barrel straight at them. Behind Dean, Marlon Spyke twirled a dagger, ready to make good on Skinner's threat. Dean stepped out onto the bowsprit and held up the vial of the Blood of Poseidon. He prayed Mookergwog would recognize him, and what he carried, before sending off a warning shot.

"Mookergwog! Open in the name of Poseidon!" he called out.

Dean held his breath as long, agonizing seconds passed. If a cannon were to sound, it would be the last thing he ever heard. Fortunately, the cannons of Aquatica remained silent. The gun barrel drooped downward, and soon after, the round castle gate slid open.

Dean turned around to face Skinner. "What'd I tell you? Nothing to worry about."

CHAPTER 28

PARLEY

Inside Aquatica, Dean sat at a round table with Skinner, Gentleman Jim, Verrick, and Mookergwog. Skinner's two best mates, Marlon Spyke and Long Tom Cannon, stood behind their captain. They didn't have a seat at the table, but they were in on the conversation—or would be, once the conversation started. At the moment, no one was talking.

All eyes were on Mookergwog, whose own eyes were fixed on the vial containing the Blood of Poseidon. Dean had presented it to him upon entering the castle. Mookergwog studied it with equal parts reverence and fear. By Dean's estimation, Mookergwog was more afraid of the liquid inside the vial than he was of the pirate crew inside his home.

"Is this real?" he asked. "It can't be real. Can it?"

"It's real," Dean replied.

"I don't understand. Why do you have it?"

"That's a long story. The short version is, I stole it."

"What?" Mookergwog looked back and forth between Dean and the blood. "How?"

"Believe it or not, the 'how' was the easy part. The 'why' is a bit more complex."

Mookergwog sat hypnotized by the Blood of Poseidon a few moments more, tightening his grip on the vial. The shock was wearing off and the severity of Dean's crime sinking in. "You violated the sacred chamber of Poseidon? This is blasphemy!"

"Actually, it's treason," Dean replied. "The queen's nephew put me up to it."

Mookergwog's eyebrows went up. "Lord Finneus?"

"The very same. He's trying to steal the throne. Duke Shellheart is helping him. After Finneus takes over, he's going to let Neptune declare war on Abyssal."

Mookergwog paled. "That can't be."

"It can be. It is. Finneus wanted to kill the queen, but that didn't work, so he made a play for the blood instead. That's where I came in."

Mookergwog looked down at the vial in his hand. "You double-crossed him?"

"He was going to do the same to me. I just beat him to the punch."

Mookergwog was starting to sweat. "If what you say is true, they'll be coming after you. Coming here."

"Can you help us?"

"Help you?" Mookergwog's breath quickened. "Help you how? I'm no warrior. I'm a clerk who likes to tinker."

"I'm *lost*," Skinner said. "What are you lot goin' on about? Why's this bloody potion so important? What is it? What's it do?"

"The Blood of Poseidon is no mere potion," Mookergwog said. "It's a bona fide miracle. One of the Great Wonders of the Sea! The slightest touch transforms man into merman, and merman back into man. If you drink it and the sea god deems you worthy, you will be blessed with his power."

Skinner scratched at his chin. "Miracles, eh?" He blew a sharp snort of air out through his nostrils. "When I was a lad, I drank the wine in church once or twice. They said that was blood too, but I know wine when I taste it. Never filled me up with no Holy Spirit, either. I don't believe in miracles. Let's talk treasure."

"This is more valuable than any treasure," Mookergwog said. "This is the power to control every fish in the sea. The greatest, most unstoppable navy in the world."

"Really?" Skinner looked over his shoulder at Spyke and Long Tom Cannon. "What do ya think, lads?"

"I think he believes it enough for all of us," Marlon Spyke said, twirling his blade.

Long Tom Cannon shrugged. "S'worth a try, isn't it?"

"So it is." Skinner turned back around and motioned for the vial. "All right, ya convinced me. Let's have a taste."

Mookergwog clutched the vial to his breast, appalled.

"You're not drinking it," Gentleman Jim said. "None of us are."

Skinner frowned. "There you go again, giving orders. Get it straight, Captain Harper." He said Harper's name like the words put a bad taste in his mouth. "Just 'cause I'm playin' nice at this here parley, don't make you the boss of me. You got a crew with one wee lad, one old geezer, and whatever you want to call Greeny here. My crew's fifty killers strong. If I decide I want something, there ain't nothin' you can do ta keep it from me."

"The power doesn't last," Dean said. "The queen has to drink that blood every month to keep it going."

"If that potion's real, one month'll be plenty. In that time, I could own the Caribbean."

"Only the royal family can drink the Blood of Poseidon," Mookergwog said. "If the contents of this vial passed your lips, it would drive you mad—at best. At worst, it would kill you. Such power isn't meant for the likes of us."

Skinner's eyes narrowed. "Yer makin' that part up."

"There's one way to find out," Gentleman Jim said. "You a gambling man, Skinner?"

"Sometimes," Skinner said with a scowl. "One thing I ain't never been is a patient man. Seaborne promised me gold. So far, I ain't seen any."

"It's down there," Dean said, pointing to the water. "It's all down there."

"How did we get to this point?" Mookergwog asked Dean. "They can't really mean to start a war, can they? Atlantis is about bringing people together."

"On the surface, maybe," Dean said. "Once you go deeper, nothing's what it seems. Not us, not Galen Fishback—he's dead, by the way—and not the honorable Lord Finneus either. He had Fishback hire assassins instead of performers the last time he came up." Dean turned to Skinner. "Those were the men you raided, the ones we replaced. They were hired to kill the queen of Atlantis. They would have done it, too, if you hadn't done them in first."

"That much I believe," Skinner said. "They were a tough lot for a group of theater types."

Dean turned back to Mookergwog. "When we showed up here, you said we were late. That was because Skinner's interference delayed Fishback's assassins—or delayed me, Ronan, and Waverly, once we replaced them. The waiting around must have gotten to Fishback, because he got cold feet. He was going to tell Captain Lyndra everything, but they killed him before he could do it."

"Fishback's body was found in Lyndra's quarters," Gentleman Jim said. "Finneus and Shellheart would have framed her for the murder, but I knew she didn't do it. That's why I took the blame. To protect her."

Dean turned toward Gentleman Jim in surprise. "That's why you confessed? To save Lyndra?"

"I had to buy her time to find out who the real villain was."

"By going to jail for life? Are you mad?"

Gentleman Jim thought it over. "Maybe a little."

"More than a little! How'd you know for sure that she was innocent?"

"I knew. She was with me when Fishback got himself killed."

"With you?"

Gentleman Jim raised an eyebrow. The realization struck Dean like lightning.

"You mean . . . you and her?" he asked Gentleman Jim.

Gentleman Jim shrugged. "Like he said, Atlantis is all about bringing people together."

Dean was gobsmacked. Skinner cackled. "Ain't love grand? The good cap'n bagged himself a fish bride!" Skinner roared with laughter and his men joined in. Dean thought Gentleman Jim and Skinner might come to blows, but the ugly pirate stopped laughing and slapped an open palm on the table. "Enough! Let's talk about bringing me together with my gold. You say it's down there. That's one place it don't do me—or you—any good. How do we get it up here?"

"We have to go back," Dean said.

"We have to save Waverly and Ronan," Verrick added, speaking up for the first time.

"Don't forget the queen," said Mookergwog. "We have to stop this war before it starts. The alternative is too horrible to contemplate."

"Cap'n!" One of Skinner's men called down to him from the walls of Aquatica. "Something just surfaced in the water to the east!"

"What is it? What's comin' up?" he hollered back.

"I don't know! Some kind of ship!"

Mookergwog sunk in his chair. "We may already be too late."

CHAPTER 29

TIDES OF WAR

The ship that surfaced in the east was not part of Shellheart's fleet but rather a lone pod-ship carrying Ronan. He came out of the Waterway closer to Aquatica than Dean and Gentleman Jim had, but he was still a good ways off. It was too far for Ronan to swim, but not too far for Dean and Gentleman Jim. Once they realized who was inside the pod, they dove into the water and together pushed Ronan's craft safely into port. When he emerged from the pod, his first order of business was a proper reunion with his former captain.

Ronan threw his arms around Gentleman Jim. "I don't care if you remember me or not. I'm just blasted happy you made it out."

Gentleman Jim patted his back. "How could I forget my first mate? You know me better than that."

Ronan looked up. "So you're back?"

"I'm back."

Dean came in to put an arm around Ronan. "It's good to have you back too. I was afraid that sponge monster was going to smother you."

"It tried," Ronan assured Dean. "Fortunately, we came to an understanding."

"I'll bet you did," Dean smirked. He had a pretty good idea how Ronan had made himself understood. "How did you get away?"

"I didn't. They let me go."

"Just you?" Verrick asked. "What about Waverly?"

"Verrick!" Ronan embraced him next. "I'm sorry. I begged them to send her up instead of me, but they wouldn't do it."

"Who's *they*?" Dean asked. "Finneus and Shellheart?"

"Aye. They want the Blood of Poseidon back. Said they'd trade us Waverly for what you stole, but that's as much as I know about this mess. I hope you didn't use it all getting out."

Dean shook his head. "We didn't, but—"

"Good." Ronan ran a hand through his hair. "That's a relief. What happened to you, mate? We thought you were half dead. Next thing we knew, you were all-the-way-gone!"

"I'm sorry, Ronan. I didn't mean to leave you behind. I was trying to save everyone." Dean grimaced. "It didn't go so well."

Ronan looked around at Skinner and his crew of cutthroats. "You can say that again."

"Trust me. It's worse than you think."

Over the next few minutes, Dean told Ronan what was really going on with Finneus. How he and Shellheart planned to overthrow the queen and start a war. How they had killed Fishback to keep it a secret, and had nearly killed Dean, not once, but twice. The whole time Dean was talking, Ronan's jaw was on the floor.

"If Finneus gets his hands on the Blood of Poseidon, there's no telling how many more will die," Mookergwog said. "We can't let him have it."

"What do you suggest we do?" Verrick asked pointedly. "There's a girl still down there. A girl I'm responsible for."

"We're going to get her back," Dean told Verrick. "I promise."

"You can't trade the Blood of Poseidon for her life," Mookergwog said. "The last time Neptune and Abyssal went to war, the ocean turned red with blood. Imagine the next time, with Atlantis joining the fight instead of stopping it. You don't know what kinds of horrors lurk in the deep places of the world. The ocean would be all but uncrossable for anyone—above the waves or below."

"The blood . . . ," Dean said. "That's it. We have to use the blood."

Mookergwog huffed. "I told you, you can't drink it. You'll go mad."

"I didn't say we should drink it."

"What are you talking about, Seaborne?" Ronan asked Dean.

"I'm talking about the one advantage we've got. Finneus thinks we're alone up here with Mookergwog. He doesn't know we've got a crew of murdering scoundrels with us."

"Heh!" Skinner laughed. "I was wonderin' when you were gonna come back 'round ta me. Here's where yer wrong. *I've* got a crew of murdering scoundrels. *You* ain't got nothin'. My men don't work for free. You were supposed to get me my fortune, Seaborne. Remember our deal?"

"The deal was to get you into Aquatica," Dean said. "I've done that. If you want your fortune, you're going to have to work for it. There's gold down there. I've seen it."

Skinner rubbed the scruff on his chin. "How much gold?"

"More than you can possibly imagine."

"I can imagine quite a lot," Skinner said. "You have a plan to get me that gold?"

"Haven't you been paying attention? The queen of Atlantis is about to be knocked off her throne. If you help save her, she'll give you a bigger reward than you could ever steal."

"I don't know, I can steal quite a lot too."

"But can you get it out? Back up here?"

Skinner thought about that for a moment. "You make a good point," he said, nodding reluctantly. "I'll ask ya one last time. What's the plan?"

"That depends. Mookergwog, you said you like to tinker?"

Mookergwog put his thumb and forefinger close together. "A bit."

"And you mixed the explosives outside this castle, didn't you? The mines?"

"I did."

"Any chance you've got the ingredients here to do a bit more?"

Mookergwog nodded. "I've got all kinds of ingredients in my workshop."

Dean grinned a crooked grin. "Let's you and I go have a look. I've got an idea."

CHAPTER 30

JUST ADD WATER

Dean rode the Waterways back to Atlantis with a newfound appreciation for the smooth, comfortable ride that a pod-ship afforded its passengers. Together with Mookergwog and Gentleman Jim, he coursed through the depths in silence. The current flipped the three of them around in every possible direction as it carried them from warm to freezing water and back again. No one said a word. Everyone was far more concerned with what lay ahead.

Soon Atlantis was in sight. The pod exited the Waterway and coasted toward the city. There was no Abyssian commando to pull them off course this time. The ship hit the Heavy Water barrier and rolled, eventually coming to rest at the edge of the main plaza. The trio stepped out of the pod and were greeted by a battalion of soldiers clad in the golden armor of Neptune.

"Hmph," Gentleman Jim grunted. "Quite a different welcome than the one I got last time."

"Not me," Dean said. "Well, it's a shinier welcome, but the sentiment is the same."

"Look there," Mookergwog said, as Finneus and Shellheart pushed through the line of soldiers. They stood at the center of the formation, waiting for Dean and his mates to make their move.

"Let's go," Dean said.

Dean, Mookergwog, and Gentleman Jim walked to the center of the plaza. Shellheart's men stayed put as he and Finneus went forth to meet them halfway.

"Welcome back," Finneus said, with the smug confidence of a person who greatly outnumbered his enemies. "I see you brought friends. Not enough to matter."

"Who is this?" Shellheart asked, pointing at Mookergwog.

"No one important," Finneus explained. "Just the customs clerk from Aquatica."

"And a loyal citizen of Atlantis," Mookergwog replied. "Unlike yourself."

"Atlantis is changing," said Finneus. "I'd advise you to change with it."

The soldiers behind Finneus and Shellheart stood with spears in hand, waiting for the order to attack.

"None of these men have the slightest idea what's happening here, do they?" asked Dean.

"They know enough," Shellheart replied. "They know you desecrated the chamber of Poseidon. Sacrilege. They also know Captain Lyndra used you to get her hands on the sacred blood. She did us all a favor by helping you escape. It's going to be even easier to start the war now."

"Where is Lyndra?" Gentleman Jim asked.

"Locked up, along with her men. I'm afraid she won't be riding to your rescue this time," Finneus said. "My aunt, of course, wants to see evidence of their involvement, but she won't be queen much longer, will she? When I'm king, everyone will simply have to take my word about Lyndra's treachery."

Dean frowned, remembering Queen Avenel's words. *Some people hardly need any reason at all to go to war.*

"My men are very good at following orders," Shellheart said. "Trust me, they'll march into battle with great big smiles on their faces."

"No they won't," Dean said. "I came here to tell you to your face you're going to lose. You're never going to be king, Finneus. It's not happening."

Finneus found Dean's bravado amusing. "Once I drink the blood, I'll be master of an endless army. King by divine right. Those who won't bow down before me will quickly learn the price of their defiance. If you don't mind your tongue, so will you."

"I'm just telling you the truth. Someone down here has to. You see, there's a problem with your plan." Dean made a show of checking his pockets and coming up empty. "I didn't bring the blood with me."

Finneus stared at Dean, stone-faced. "I'm not in the mood for jokes."

"You think I'm joking? See for yourself."

"Search him," Finneus told Shellheart. "Search all of them."

Dean, Mookergwog, and Gentleman Jim allowed the duke to search them one by one. When Shellheart came up dry, Finneus appeared ready to erupt. "What are you doing? Surely, you realize giving me the blood is your only hope of getting your friend out of here alive."

"Where is Waverly?" Dean asked. "What have you done with her?"

"She's in the palace. And I haven't done anything yet, but if you don't stop playing games . . ."

"Don't worry, the blood's coming. But you might not be happy when it gets here."

"What are you talking about?"

"Tell me something while we wait. If you wanted to be king so badly, why didn't you just go get the blood yourself? All that power, practically unguarded . . . you didn't need me. You didn't need him," Dean said, indicating the duke. "You could have just taken care of it on your own. Why didn't you? The truth is, you didn't have the guts."

Finneus balked at Dean's accusation. "I didn't want to tempt the sea god's wrath."

"Oh, that's right, I forgot. You're a righteous merman. Same reason you had to hire out the killing of your aunt. Couldn't get your hands dirty there, either. If you do it, you're a blasphemer. If I do it, you're in the clear."

Finneus nodded. "Something like that."

"Something like that?" Dean laughed. "You think the sea god, assuming he really exists, can't see through your lies? You think he's fooled?" Dean stopped smiling and leaned in close to Finneus's face. "You really think he's going to find you worthy?"

"I *am* worthy." Finneus pushed Dean back. "You'll see."

"If you say so."

Just then, another pod broke through the Heavy Water barrier. It rolled onto the plaza floor and came to rest a few feet away from where Dean and the others stood.

Finneus was not impressed. "Who's in there? Your friend Ronan, the fighter?"

Dean nodded. "Among others."

Finneus rolled his eyes. The pod held four people at most. "Am I supposed to be scared?"

The pod split in half, opening up like a locket. A monstrous tidal wave of water poured out. It was as if a caged ocean had been loosed upon the city. Finneus gasped. Shellheart staggered back. "The pod . . . it's filled with DeepWater!"

The same enchanted water that Waverly had used in her high dive act came rolling across the plaza, strong enough to crush everything in its path.

"Not just DeepWater," said Dean. Swimming inside the massive wave were Ronan, Verrick, Skinner, and the full crew of the *Crimson Tide*. They had all been transformed into mermen for the journey. "I told you to be careful what you wished for. You wanted blood. Now you're gonna get it."

CHAPTER 31

BLOOD AND GUTS

The wave hit like a fast moving mountain, scattering Shellheart's forces. The soldiers of Neptune tried to run, but it was no use. A flash flood engulfed the plaza, surging forward and picking up everything in its path—including Dean and his friends. Riding the instant tsunami, they charged the Atlantean castle. It was the only way. A frontal assault with Shellheart's men in their path would have made for a bloody mess on both sides. Riding the wave, they were literally all in it together. The water deposited everyone on the steps of the palace.

Dean rolled over on his back. All around him, soldiers in golden armor were piled up in heaps, their weapons strewn across the plaza. Finneus and Shellheart lay a few feet off, trapped beneath a mound of stunned soldiers.

Skinner hobbled over to Dean, sloshing through puddles with his wet boot and waterlogged stump. "I gotta hand it to ya, Seaborne. Yer plan worked." He leaned against the palace wall for support and offered Dean a hand up. "I'm impressed. Walkin' in here without so much as a sword at yer side? Ya got guts."

"He's walked into worse situations," Ronan said, coming up behind Skinner.

"Let's not get ahead of ourselves," Dean said, picking up a sword one of Shellheart's men had lost in the deluge. "This isn't over yet."

"You don't have to tell me," Skinner agreed. "On yer feet, scalawags! Step lively!"

Skinner's crew forced themselves to stand and draw their swords. They seemed to be recovering faster than the soldiers of Neptune, maybe because they didn't want to incur their captain's wrath. Or maybe starting out inside the wave wasn't quite as bad as getting hit by it. A few Neptunians staggered to their feet, but Skinner's men quickly knocked them back down. It wasn't long before the crew of the *Crimson Tide* had taken the fight out of every one of Shellheart's soldiers. When the brief, one-sided battle was over, the pirates wandered about with their mouths open, marveling at the city and the Heavy Water barrier that covered it.

"All right, lads. Keep moving," Skinner said, pointing to the palace gate. "Eyes on the prize. We ain't here ta see the blasted sights."

"You wasted the blood on these men?" Finneus said, aghast.

"Gave myself a fresh dose too," Dean said. "Hope you don't mind."

Finneus clawed his way out from under the pile of armored soldiers. "I'm going to kill you for this."

"Come and get me," Dean said.

He turned his back on Finneus and went inside the palace. Skinner, his crew, Ronan, Gentleman Jim, Mookergwog, and Verrick all followed. Verrick stumbled on his way in the door, and Gentleman Jim caught him. "Are you all right, old-timer?"

"I'm fine," Verrick said, wresting himself from Gentleman Jim's helping hands. The journey to Atlantis had taxed him, but he was not without his pride.

"You're sure?" Ronan asked.

"I am," Verrick assured him. "I was just momentarily overwhelmed . . . by all of this." He motioned to the castle and the city outside the door. "I still don't understand how we got here, or how you managed to fit so much water in that pod."

"That was nothing," Mookergwog said. "Wasn't even half a barrel's worth of DeepWater."

"It's a good thing you had all that stuff topside," Ronan said.

"I needed something to pass the time up there," Mookergwog replied. "Lucky for you, I like to keep myself busy."

"Aye, let's see some more 'a' yer handiwork," Skinner said. "Mr. Spyke! Got that bag I told ya ta look after?"

"Right here, Cap'n." Marlon Spyke held up a drenched leather satchel. Glass bottles clinked together inside it.

"Careful with that!" warned Mookergwog. "Those bottles are filled with the same ingredients as my mines. If one of them breaks . . ."

"At ease, Greeny," Skinner said. "Marlon Spyke's got the surest hands in the seven seas. You ought to see what he can do with a blade."

"If we're lucky, we won't," Dean said.

Skinner smirked. "Somethin' tells me you and 'lucky' don't mix."

"Fire in the hole!" shouted Long Tom Cannon, holding up one of the glass bottles. Marlon Spyke, who had just finished stacking the other bottles around the door, scurried away. Everyone found cover and plugged their ears as Long Tom threw his bottle as hard as he could. It smashed into the bottles on the floor, and the resulting explosion nearly brought the house down. Boulder-sized chunks of wall piled up in the doorway, blocking the entrance to the palace.

Once the dust had settled, Long Tom Cannon kicked at the base of the rock pile. The barricade was good and strong. "That should hold them," Long Tom said. "For a time."

"Time enough for us to reach the queen," Skinner said. "Where do we find 'er, Seaborne?"

Dean pointed down a long hallway. "Throne room. That way."

"Well? What're ya waiting for, ya bunch 'a' barnacles? Let's go earn that treasure!" Skinner's crew whooped and hollered as the men charged down the hall.

Mookergwog frowned once Skinner had disappeared around the corner. "I don't like him."

"None of us like him," said Dean. "We just happen to need him."

"We need more than just him," said Gentleman Jim. "Lyndra and her men. They can help us if we can find out where they're being held."

"I'll go with you," Ronan said. "There's someone else I have to break out."

"Go," Dean urged him. "We owe Lyndra that much and more."

Verrick touched Dean's shoulder. "I owe a duty to Waverly's father. You and I must find her."

Dean nodded. That went without saying.

"I'll head to the throne room," Mookergwog said. "The queen needs to know what's happening here. Someone has to tell her about her nephew."

The sound of rowdy pirates echoed through the palace. "Someone needs to keep an eye on Skinner too," Dean said. "We'll join you as soon as we can."

"With backup," Gentleman Jim added.

Mookergwog gave a worried nod and started down the hall alone. "Hurry."

After he was gone, Gentleman Jim and Ronan went off to find the dungeons.

"Where should you and I start looking?" Verrick asked.

Dean spied one of the queen's royal stewards. "Let's ask him," Dean suggested. He and Verrick cornered the man.

"Where is the princess being held?" Verrick asked him, taking out his sword.

"Who?" the steward asked, trembling.

"The human girl who came here with me," Dean said. "The diver. The princess of peril? There's only one human girl in the city, blast it!"

"She's in the west wing!" the steward said.

"Let's go," Verrick said, sheathing his sword.

Moving westward, Verrick and Dean found the wing to be a maze of halls and guest rooms. They split up to find Waverly faster. Dean checked empty room after empty room, but in the fifth room, someone blindsided him. A hard blow to the head saw him dropped to the floor. When he rolled over onto his back, he looked up to find Waverly standing over him, holding a candlestick.

"Dean!?" she said. "What are you doing here?"

"Nnnng!" Dean said, rubbing the back of his head. "What do you think? I'm here for you."

Waverly put the candlestick down. "I heard the explosions and thought a war had broken out. I should have known it was you." She helped Dean up. Once he was back on his feet, she slapped him in the face.

"Ow!" Dean shouted. "What was that for?"

"That was for choosing Gentleman Jim's life over Verrick's. Do you realize what you've done? He's out of time. We'll never save him now."

She slapped him again. "Ow!"

"And that was for leaving me and Ronan behind!"

"Waverly, stop!" Dean said, clutching his cheek. "I didn't have a choice."

"That's what you always say."

"It's true! I didn't want to leave. I had to. Finneus would have killed me otherwise."

That got Waverly's attention. "What?"

"You heard me. By the way, it must've been terrible for you. This is some prison you're in." Dean motioned to the luxurious suite surrounding them. The west wing of the palace was clearly meant for royal guests.

"I'm not a prisoner! Finneus has been doing everything he can to make me comfortable since you ran out and abandoned me here."

"Is that what he told you? Waverly, come on . . . You've been looking at me different ever since we left Port Royal, but do you really think I'd leave you here to die?"

"I didn't, but . . ." Waverly paused. "What do you mean, leave me here to die?"

"Finneus and Shellheart are trying to overthrow the queen. I made the mistake of finding out about it and got roped into their plans. They were going to kill you if I didn't bring back the Blood of Poseidon."

"Oh," Waverly said, slightly embarrassed. "Did you give it to him?"

"Not exactly."

"Not exactly! Are you trying to get me killed?"

"It's complicated," Dean stressed. "I'll tell you everything, I promise, but right now I need you to trust me."

"Now that sounds like a risky proposition," Waverly said, coming around. Her lips had the trace of a smile.

"Maybe," Verrick said, standing in the door. "But you never needed anyone's help to risk your life."

"Verrick!" Waverly rushed to embrace him. "You saved him after all," she said to Dean.

"*Saved* is a strong word," Dean said. "None of us are out of danger yet."

"Aye," Verrick agreed. "But I'm relieved to find you safe for the moment. I haven't been much of a guardian these past few days."

"No," said Waverly. "It was just my turn to make sure you stayed alive."

"We need to do the same for Queen Avenel," Dean said. "Now that all his plans are falling apart, there's no telling what Finneus will do."

"Where's Ronan?" asked Waverly. "Is he with the queen?"

"No, Skinner's guarding her."

Waverly's mouth fell open. "Skinner! Are you mad?"

Dean smirked. "Isn't that obvious? Come on, I'll explain on the way."

CHAPTER 32

God Save the Queen

When Dean, Waverly, and Verrick arrived in the throne room, they found that they had been right to worry about Skinner. The pirates had subdued the queen's guards, and Queen Avenel herself was being held at the point of a knife. Mookergwog stood next to her, guarded by Marlon Spyke and Long Tom Cannon. Skinner sat on the shell-shaped throne, covered in jewels and directing his men with a diamond-tipped scepter as they carried chests of gold out of the treasure vault.

"Seaborne!" Skinner said, beaming. "Glad you could make it. You were right, lad. This here's the haul of a lifetime!"

"Skinner, you idiot!" Dean shouted. "You were supposed to protect the queen. Not rob her!"

"In return for a share of her treasure, yes. But I gots ta thinkin'... what if One-Eyed Jack had the right idea about sharing, after all? I said ta meself, 'Self, why settle for a taste when you can take the whole blasted thing?'"

"That wasn't the deal," Dean said.

"You were counting on me to stick to the deal? Ha! Now who's the idiot?"

"You are, if you think you're going to make it out of that chair," Finneus called out. He stepped through the main entrance with Shellheart at his side and a regiment of soldiers at his back. Every man jack of them was itching for a fight. Believing they had come to her rescue, the queen looked immensely relieved to see them. Dean knew that feeling wouldn't last.

"Just keepin' it warm for ya, guv'nor." Skinner hoisted himself up and stood next to the throne, patting the seat cushion. "From what I understand, you've got designs on this seat, but yer a mite squeamish when it comes ta knocking off queenie here. Is that right?"

The room went quiet.

"Finneus, what's he talking about?" asked the queen.

"Myself, I don't have that particular problem," Skinner continued. "The way I see it, there's no need for the two of us ta be at odds. Not when we can work this out to each other's benefit."

Finneus approached the steps of the royal dais. "Go on."

"Finneus!" Queen Avenel exclaimed. "What are you doing?"

"Oh, shut up, Aunt Avenel," Finneus snapped. "Are you really so surprised?"

The queen was devastated. "Are you really so impatient to rule that you would usurp me? I have no other heirs . . . you were already in line to be king!"

"But *when*?" Finneus demanded. "How long did you expect me to run your insipid human circus? Putting on shows so these monkeys can dance for our amusement? It's beneath me!"

"Oh, Finneus." The queen paused to wipe a tear from her eye. "You poor, misguided boy. Duke Shellheart, please stop this madness."

"I'm afraid you're wasting your breath, Your Majesty," Duke Shellheart replied, coming forward to join Finneus. "If you want to talk about madness, start with the decision to host soldiers from Neptune and Abyssal in the same city and then expect us to keep the peace. It's unnatural, and I'm afraid it can no longer be tolerated."

Shellheart appeared relieved to finally voice his contempt for the truce, but Dean saw the soldiers behind him looked conflicted and confused. "I thought it was Captain Lyndra trying to steal the throne," he heard one of them say. Sir Riptide, the scar-faced soldier who had nearly lost his eye to an Abyssian "savage," told the men to keep their mouths shut and stay in formation. They did as they were told, but there was dissension in their ranks.

Dean wasn't the only one who saw it. Skinner banged the scepter in his hand against the back of the throne, grabbing everyone's attention before more soldiers started thinking for themselves.

"Here's the deal!" Skinner hollered. "Finneus! Shellheart! You let me and mine walk out of here with as much treasure as we can carry, and in return, I'll take yer queen so far away that not even her ghost will ever find its way back ta haunt ya. You don't have ta lift a finger. Just let us pass and we can all get what we want. It don't matter ta me what goes on down here. My life's up above the waves."

"What about them?" Finneus asked, pointing to Dean, Waverly, and Verrick.

"Keep 'em. Kill 'em. What do I care?"

Finneus gave a shrug. "Works for me."

"Not for me," Gentleman Jim called out from across the room.

"Or me," said Lyndra, standing beside him, backed by a regiment of Abyssian soldiers. "Neither thief nor traitor will walk out of this room. You're all going to have to be carried out."

"Who are *they*?" Skinner asked, pointing to Lyndra's men in their black crustacean armor.

Shellheart smiled. "The soldiers I've spent my life waiting to fight."

"You can't!" said the queen. "The war's been over for a hundred years! Are you mad?"

Shellheart shook his head. "Wars are never really over, Your Majesty. Hatred can endure for generations." He turned to his men. "Sons of Neptune! Today, you honor your fathers and your fathers' fathers . . . all those who fell in battle to Abyssal shall be avenged."

"Stand down!" ordered the queen. "I beg you!"

Shellheart's men seemed unsure who to obey, the duke or the queen. Dean seized the moment before it passed. "Wait!" he shouted, running to stand in between the two armies. "You don't have to fight. Finneus, you told me if I gave you the blood, no one had to die."

"That was before," Finneus said. "You squandered that chance when you gave the blood to this scum."

"Not all of it." Dean held up a vial. It was still half full.

The throne room let out a collective gasp. Every merman and mermaid present stared at the blood with reverent eyes.

"Where did that come from?" Finneus asked.

"I searched you!" Shellheart said. "Where did you hide it?"

"I didn't hide it. I didn't even have it. Ronan brought it down in the second pod."

"You said you used it all," Finneus said.

"I lied," Dean said. "I do that. How about you? You said you were worthy. Don't you want to find out if it's true?"

CHAPTER 33

BAD BLOOD

"Don't!" Lyndra blurted. "You can't let him have the blood. You don't understand its power."

"It's all right," Queen Avenel said, still at the mercy of Marlon Spyke's knife. "Go ahead, young man," she told Dean. "Give it to him. Let's see what happens. Let everyone see."

"Queen Avenel!" Lyndra exclaimed. "You can't mean that. You can't let him have the power of the—"

"Finneus will draw no power from the blood, Captain," said the queen, cutting Lyndra off. "He has already proven himself to be unworthy."

"Of course you would say that," Finneus scowled. "You think so little of me. That's why you only ever trusted me with trivialities."

The queen scoffed. "I would have been right not to trust you. But the truth is, I made you minister of cultural exchange because I thought highly of you. Even a queen makes mistakes—but Lord Poseidon does not. I submit to the will of the sea god, as do we all. Let his judgment reveal the truth about you, dear nephew. Drink freely. We shall all bear witness. If Poseidon sees fit to give you command over all sea life, I will obey you as I would him."

Finneus's eyebrows went up. "Will you? I had no idea you would be so accommodating. We should have had this conversation long ago." He joined Dean on the steps. "You all heard her. The queen freely offers me to drink the Blood of Poseidon."

"I wouldn't drink that, lad," Skinner warned Finneus. "I wouldn't drink anything one 'a' my enemies offered me. Not a drop. Leave it alone. Ya can be king without it."

"Not here, he can't," Dean said. "If he wants to be king of Atlantis, he needs the sea god's blessing. He needs His power."

"And I will have it," Finneus said, taking the vial from Dean. "This is no crime. This is mine by right."

"Keep telling yourself that," Dean said.

Finneus stared at the white liquid in the bottle as if hypnotized. "The Blood of Poseidon," he said in awe. "Dominion over the waves—mine at last." He raised the vial, toasting the future. "The new age of Atlantis begins now!"

Finneus downed the vial in one gulp. The throne room fell

silent. The young lord closed his eyes and breathed easy, waiting for his transformation and the power that would come with it.

Nothing happened.

A few seconds passed as Finneus felt nervously at his arms and chest, still expecting to receive the sea god's blessing. "I don't understand."

"Something's wrong," one of Shellheart's soldiers said.

"Just as I suspected," said the queen. "Unworthy."

"I'm not unworthy!" Finneus growled. "Stop saying that!" He staggered a step, briefly losing his balance on the staircase. After he steadied himself, he put a hand to his head and looked around the throne room. There was fear in his eyes.

"You feel it?" Dean asked him. "Is the room spinning yet?"

In that moment, Finneus realized Dean had played him. "You did this. You tricked me!" He grabbed Dean and threw him down the stairs.

"He's been poisoned," Shellheart shouted as Dean rolled to a stop at his feet. "This is treachery—foul treachery!"

"Yes, Duke Shellheart," the scar-faced Sir Riptide agreed.

"Kill the boy," Shellheart said. "Let him be the first to die."

Sir Riptide drew his sword. "No, Duke Shellheart."

The Duke whirled on him. "What did you say?"

"The sea god has judged Lord Finneus . . . and you. I will not wage war on Abyssal unprovoked, nor take up arms against the rightful queen."

"You dare defy me?" Shellheart said, drawing his own sword. "Your cowardice shames all of Neptune."

"My only shame is that I waited this long to act. Forgive me, my queen. The duke's treason ends here."

Shellheart flew into a rage and swung his sword at Riptide. A mighty clang rang out as it connected with his golden shield. Halfway up the steps, Finneus stared in disbelief as, one by one, Shellheart's soldiers turned on their duke—and him. As more of Shellheart's men came forth to challenge him, Mookergwog took advantage of the confusion and threw his weight into Marlon Spyke, knocking the pirate off the royal dais.

"The queen is unguarded!" Lyndra shouted. "Defend her!"

"Save the queen!" Riptide told his men while trading blows with Shellheart.

The soldiers of Abyssal charged, and the battle began, but not the one Finneus and Shellheart had hoped for. A wave of black and gold armor came together to fight side by side against Skinner's men.

"Bloody 'ell!" Skinner cursed. "Looks like we'll have ta fight our way out of here after all. Have at 'em, lads! If ya want ta keep yer treasure, yer gonna have ta kill every one 'a' these blasted fish-men!"

The pirate crew ran headlong into the fray. But this time, they not only lacked the element of surprise, they were up against two armies instead of one. They had no hope of winning, and Skinner knew it. As Dean went back up the stairs to the royal dais, he passed Skinner and Long Tom Cannon, headed down.

"Grab Spyke and as much gold as you can carry," Skinner ordered Long Tom. "We're out of here. Now."

Before Dean could tell Skinner he should have stuck to the plan, a fist collided with Dean's face. He shook his head clear and saw Finneus, looking feverish and desperate.

"What did you give me?" he demanded, with sweat beading up on his brow. "What did I drink?"

Dean spat blood and smiled. "I'm not sure exactly. I can tell you this much, it wasn't the Blood of Poseidon. Verrick held what was left of that, not Ronan."

"*Who?*"

Dean nodded up to the dais. "See the old man whisking your aunt away to safety?" Finneus turned around in time to see Verrick escorting the queen out through a side entrance. When he turned back around, Dean head-butted him in the nose. Finneus cried out, and both of them fell.

"Don't worry," Dean said, crawling to his feet. "He gave the blood to Waverly to hold."

"Over here," Waverly said, crossing the steps to kick Finneus in the chest. "I have met some low-down liars in my day," she told him, "but you top them all."

"And here I thought I was going to be stuck with that title," Dean joked.

Finneus rolled over in pain. He looked weak and washed-out. "What was it? Poison? Am I going to die?"

"Die?" Mookergwog repeated. "No, that was just a little potion I use to help me go to sleep. Not to worry, I've used it myself many times with no side effects. Though it does a smoother job if you don't fight it."

"Hear that?" Dean asked. "You're going to go to bed soon, and when you wake up, you'll be in prison."

"Liar," Finneus spat. "Cheat!"

"I *told* you I was a liar," Dean said. "Weren't you paying attention?"

At the base of the steps, Shellheart was matching swords with Lyndra and Gentleman Jim, and he was losing. On the floor of the throne room, the combined forces of Neptune and Abyssal had overwhelmed the pirates—with the notable exception of their captain, Long Tom, and Spyke. The trio was about to make its escape when a giant sponge monster blocked the men's path.

"Skinner!" Ronan said, appearing next to the sponge creature. "Good to see you. I'd like you to meet a friend of mine."

The sponge monster roared and swiped at Skinner, Marlon Spyke, and Long Tom Cannon. The three of them flew into the throne room wall hard enough to crack the stone facade. The impact scattered the treasure they'd stolen, and Ronan put a hand up to shield himself as he was pelted with gold coins. "Ah! Were those pirates or piñatas?" The sponge monster groaned out an unintelligible reply.

"Blow me down," Dean marveled. "He really did come to an understanding with that thing."

Ronan threw Dean and Waverly a salute as he and the sponge monster joined the battle. It would all be over soon.

"It can't end this way," Finneus muttered, fighting the urge to sleep. "I won't allow it!" He forced himself onto his feet and charged up the steps.

"Where does he think he's going?" Dean asked.

"After the queen?" Mookergwog guessed.

"Look," Waverly said, pointing. Finneus picked up a sword and darted through the secret door behind the throne.

"He's headed for Poseidon's Chamber," Dean said.

"After him!" Mookergwog shouted.

Dean, Mookergwog, and Waverly ran after Finneus. The waterfall on the back wall of the throne room drenched them as they ran under it, chasing Finneus into the treasure vault. He didn't get far. They found him a short ways down the winding staircase below the vault. He was sitting with his back against the massive tank of pressurized Heavy Water. When Finneus saw that Dean and the others had caught up to him, he lifted his sword in their direction.

"Seaborne," he said, wheezing. "You robbed me of my destiny . . . my future. Now, it's my turn . . . to do the same."

Finneus swung his sword, but not at Dean. His target was a block of machinery and wires that had been bolted to the side of the water tank.

"No!" Mookergwog screamed, but it was too late. Sparks erupted from the severed cables and steam poured out from the seams of the tank as the needle on a large pressure gauge began to drop.

"What just happened?" Waverly asked. "What did he do?"

"I'm not going to rot in some prison," Finneus said. "I'll take this city down with me first."

CHAPTER 34

DOWNFALL

"He killed the power," Mookergwog said, horrified. "He killed the power to the tank!"

"What does that mean?" Waverly asked.

Mookergwog leaned away as blue flames flared up around Finneus's sword, now wedged in the block of damaged machinery. "It means he's killed us!"

"No!" Dean reached into the flames and pulled the sword out. He tossed it aside, shaking his hands from the heat. "Don't say that. What do we do?"

Mookergwog ripped off his shirt and used it to beat out the flames. The wires and melted rubber were a charred mess. "Nothing we can do. He cut the lines. The tower won't run without power."

"What power?" Waverly asked.

Electric bolts crackled in the place where the flames had been.

"That!" Mookergwog said, pointing. "Electric power . . . There's a hydroelectric generator below the tank."

Dean squinted. "A hydro-what?" He'd been below the tank and he didn't have the first clue what Mookergwog was talking about.

Mookergwog made circles with his hands. "Giant wheels!" he barked.

"Okay," Dean nodded. That he understood.

"Falling water turns the wheels fast enough to build up energy. We need that power to pull oxygen from the water—we need it to keep the Heavy Water in this tank under pressure! Otherwise, it won't be strong enough to cover the city."

Waverly pointed up at the ceiling. "The Water Tower's going to fall?"

"Once the water stops flowing, everything's going to fall," Mookergwog said. "The ocean's going to crash down on us and wipe out all of Atlantis. We're doomed."

"Stop saying that!" Dean grabbed Mookergwog. "Blast it, Mookergwog, think! You know machines. You can fix this."

Mookergwog shook his head, afraid. "I like to build things, but that's not the same as—"

"Tell me you can fix this!"

"I don't know! Maybe I could rewire it, but—"

"Good!" Dean's face lit up. "Rewiring sounds good. Let's do that!"

"But I lack the tools!" Mookergwog continued. "Without them, it's impossible. First of all, I'd be electrocuted. Second, we don't have enough time!"

"You have to try!" Waverly pleaded.

"Look at this." Mookergwog pointed to a pressure gauge on the side of the tank. The needle on its face was moving quickly to the left. "Once that needle hits the red, it's all over. I'd need minutes to reroute the power around these two main cables. But we have seconds to reestablish that connection—at best!"

"A connection between these two cables here?" Dean asked, making sure he was looking at the right ones.

"Yes."

"Okay." Dean spit on his hands and rubbed them together. "I'll buy you as much time as I can."

"What do you mean, buy me—"

"Dean!" Waverly screamed as he reached out and grabbed the severed ends of each cable. It must have looked like suicide, but she didn't know what the queen's healers had told Dean: that merpeople were slightly more resistant to electric shocks. Slightly.

The voltage still hurt like the devil. Using his body as a conductor, Dean bridged the gap between the two severed cables. He cried out in agony, but the pressure gauge climbed slowly up out of the danger zone. It was working! Unfortunately, Mookergwog wasn't.

"What are you waiting for?" Dean shouted.

"Sorry! Right!" Mookergwog sprang into action as Dean kept a watery roof over the city's head. Dean's hands became iron claws—the pain was killing him, but he couldn't let go, even if he wanted to. He could barely move.

Dean lost track of time as Mookergwog frantically worked to fix the Water Tower. The few minutes that passed felt like a lifetime.

"Are you done yet?" he heard Waverly ask Mookergwog.

"Not yet . . ."

"Go faster!"

"Distracting me doesn't do him any good! If you want to make yourself useful, go get another merman to relieve him."

"I'll relieve him!"

"No," Mookergwog cursed and pulled his hand back. A wire he'd been splicing together had given him a nasty shock. "You're human. You'll die if you touch that. It has to be a merman."

Waverly took out what was left of the Blood of Poseidon. There were still a few drops at the bottom of the vial. "What about a *mermaid*?"

Dean looked over his shoulder at Waverly, wondering if she was the last thing he'd ever see. Mookergwog jumped back again as sparks shot out of the contraption he'd been working on.

"Power surge! Not now!" the green man shouted.

Dean screamed as the pain became unbearable, and then everything went white.

CHAPTER 35

NOT DEAD YET

Dean opened his eyes and saw nothing. Wherever he was, it was pitch-black.

"Am I dead?" he asked. His head was pounding. His body ached. He wasn't sure if he had spoken the words aloud or only thought them.

"No," a woman's voice replied.

"Not for lack of trying," said a second.

"This is getting to be a habit with you, Dean Seaborne."

"A bad habit."

Dean recognized the voices. The healers. He was back on their table. Alive.

"You humans are a crazy people," said one of the healers. "Do not take this the wrong way, Dean Seaborne, but we hope to never see you here again."

Dean propped himself up on his elbows, realizing as he did that his hands had been wrapped with bandages. "That's fine. Don't take this the wrong way, but I'm tired of waking up in here."

One of the healers—Dean could never tell one from the other—patted his head. "Try to stay out of trouble. You deserve a long life."

"We are forever in your debt," the other healer said. "Both of you."

"Both of us?" Dean asked, but the healers were already on their way out. They shut the door behind them, leaving him alone with—"Waverly?" Dean rolled over and saw her recuperating in a sick bed next to his.

"Feeling better?" she asked him.

"Look at you," Dean said, taking note of her bandaged hands.

"Good thing you gave me the blood," Waverly said with a smile. "Otherwise neither of us might be here."

"I gave you that so you could escape to the sea if you needed to. Not so you could get yourself electrocuted."

"Is that your way of saying thank you for saving your life?"

"I think I was pretty heroic there myself. Let's not forget that," Dean said playfully. "Just how long did you let me fry before you jumped in, anyway? I'm guessing you must have come in right at the end."

"Ha!" Waverly laughed. "I wish. Mookergwog told me I held out two minutes longer than you did before I blacked out."

Dean laughed back. It felt good to be laughing with Waverly again. It felt good just to be alive. "I'm glad that's over with."

"Almost. They're waiting for us."

"Who's waiting?"

Waverly smiled. "Everyone."

CHAPTER 36

Atlantean Knights

Dean and Waverly were the last to arrive in the throne room. The two of them limped in to the sound of thunderous applause. Dean winced as Ronan picked him up in a bear hug.

"Easy, Ronan! We've taken enough punishment for one day."

"Sorry." Ronan set Dean down and backed away to allow Gentleman Jim, Verrick, Mookergwog, and Lyndra to give him and Waverly a hero's welcome. Neptunians and Abyssians were standing side by side in the room, cheering for Dean and Waverly's selflessness in saving the city.

"Where's Finneus?" Waverly asked Ronan. "Not invited?"

Ronan laughed. "He's in jail with Shellheart, Skinner, and the rest of his scalawags. Not liable to get out anytime soon, either."

"When the pirates turn human again, they can have my old cell," Gentleman Jim said.

The queen cleared her throat, and the room quieted. Dean and his friends fell in line before her.

"My friends," Queen Avenel began, "today is a day of tragedy and triumph. For the past hundred years, we have had peace under the sea. A peace that, mere hours ago, was almost shattered—along with this city. Through the work of noble hearts, Atlantis lives. Peace endures. But I have come to realize that peace is not measured only by the absence of conflict. It stems from understanding. Compassion. Love for one another. These are things that, despite our best efforts, we did not have here. Perhaps we have never truly had them. After all these years, I think I know why. I must reveal a harsh truth to you. It pains me to say this, but the Atlantis you know is based on a lie."

A murmur ran through the crowd. Dean and his friends looked at each other. This was not the victory speech any of them had expected.

"You may wonder how it is I knew Lord Poseidon would deem Finneus unworthy to wield His power. It was not my faith in the sea god's wisdom that made me so sure, but rather the fact that no merman or mermaid has ever wielded such a power—myself included. The Blood of Poseidon does not grant mastery over every fish in the sea. That was all just a story. My father first told it a hundred years ago, and we've been telling it ever since."

"I don't understand," Captain Lyndra said. "That can't be."

"Believe me, it can," Queen Avenel assured everyone. "It's very simple, really. Our ancestors wanted to end the war but didn't know how. My father helped negotiate a truce between Neptune and Abyssal, but both sides were concerned about the opposing army's willingness to lay down arms. It was my father's idea to use the Blood of Poseidon as a deterrent, and thus the 'Atlantean Navy' was born. An unstoppable force, the living embodiment of the sea god's wrath, and a creative solution to a shared problem. The sea god's will became the means to convince the Mer-Realm that peace was the only alternative to annihilation."

"People wouldn't have just believed a story like that," Lyndra said. "They would have had to see it for themselves."

"They believed it because the rulers of all three cities swore that they had seen the power of the blood in action. You all believed it because you grew up hearing those stories. And why would you question it? Atlantis is filled with wonders. The transformative power of the blood is real enough. All of you here have seen its effects firsthand. Was the rest of the story any harder to swallow?"

The queen was right, Dean thought. By the time he found out about the Atlantean Navy, he had seen so many impossible things that he no longer questioned any of them.

"That means Finneus was doomed to fail," Dean said. "Everything he did to get the blood . . . even if we had given him the real thing, it would have gained him nothing."

"His plot to commandeer the storied navy—that was doomed to fail. But his plan to overthrow me by other means could have easily succeeded. He would have had me killed, if not for you."

"Queen Avenel, why are you telling us this now?" asked Captain Lyndra. "Finneus's treachery has been exposed. You could have maintained the facade. The threat is passed."

"The threat is passed today. What about tomorrow? We have been given the chance to be true to each other, and I refuse to waste it. I won't be here forever. The Atlantean Navy was a lie told for noble reasons, but it was a lie nonetheless, and a relationship cannot be built upon a lie. Communication. Trust. This is what we need now."

Dean's eyes met Waverly's. The queen might as well have been speaking about the two of them.

"Finneus was right about one thing," said the queen. "The new era of Atlantis begins today. As of this moment, the kingdoms of Neptune and Abyssal are formally released from their pledges of fealty to my throne and to the kingdom of Atlantis. Henceforth, our people shall share the sea as equals. And if we have peace— as I pray that we do—we will share responsibility for that peace together. The ocean is big enough for all of us."

The mood in the throne room was somber.

"What if it isn't?" asked the scar-faced Sir Riptide.

"It has to be," the queen said softly. "If not, we deserve our fate." She clapped her hands. "Mookergwog, keeper of Aquatica, come forth!" Mookergwog did as he was told and stepped forward. "Your talents are clearly wasted in your current occupation. Your mechanical prowess saved us all. For this reason, you shall have a place among my royal engineers as long as the kingdom stands."

"Yes, Your Majesty," Mookergwog beamed. "Thank you, Your Majesty!"

"Thank you, good sir," the queen smiled. "Captain James Harper, also known as Gentleman Jim," she called out next. "Your sentence is commuted. You are free to go—or stay, if that is your wish. It is up to you."

Gentleman Jim took Lyndra's hand in his. "I mean to stay." He turned to Lyndra. "If you'll stay here with me."

"With your permission, Your Majesty?" Lyndra asked the queen.

"It will be my honor to have you here together," the queen replied.

With that, Lyndra grabbed hold of Gentleman Jim and kissed him. Ronan's eyebrows shot up.

"He didn't mention that?" Dean asked him.

"No." Ronan shook his head and smiled at Gentleman Jim. "You old dog, you."

"And finally, we come to my three world-class daredevils," said the queen. "It seems you were even more daring than expected. Stealing the Blood of Poseidon?" she aimed a reproachful eye at Dean. "I don't recall reading that in the playbill."

"I am sorry for that," Dean said. "Hopefully, my actions are considered less sacrilegious now that we know it was not truly the blood of a god."

The queen frowned. "I never said that. The blood may not do all that the legends promised, but I have no doubt it is born of divine provenance. Poseidon works in mysterious ways. Even now, after all of this, I sense His trident in the water, shaping the current. Showing us the way. I shall include you in my prayers always and thank Him for sending you here. Without you, all would have been lost."

The queen stood up. One of her guardsmen handed her a silver sword, which she carried down the steps to Dean, Ronan, and Waverly.

"Bend thy knees."

Dean kneeled before the queen and bowed his head. His friends did the same. "For your service to my kingdom, for sacrificing your bodies to save the Water Tower . . ." The sword lightly touched Dean's shoulders as the queen spoke, then proceeded to Waverly and Ronan in turn. ". . . for your commitment to justice, for stopping the pirates who accosted me . . . I dub thee Knights of Atlantis."

Spirited shouts of approval filled the room. Dean, Ronan, and Waverly arose, humbled by the honor.

"My people," the queen began. "My *friends*. Today, we celebrate peace under the sea. I don't know what the next hundred years will hold, or tomorrow for that matter, but I have faith. Whatever the tide brings in, we will face it together."

Dean looked at Waverly. "That sounds good to me."

"Me too."

"Well then," Ronan said, putting an arm around each of them. "Where are we off to next? We're going to have to sail to the ends of the earth to top this adventure."

"Ugh," Dean grunted. "I was hoping we might take it easy for a bit."

"Exactly what I was thinking," Waverly said.

Dean double-took Waverly. "You? Take it easy? I didn't realize you knew how."

"Of course I do," Waverly said, starting toward the exit. "This is Atlantis, after all. We deserve to enjoy it." She turned to look back over her shoulder. "Care to join me for a swim?"

"Aye," Dean smiled. "I'm right behind you."

ACKNOWLEDGMENTS

So, this book you're holding . . . it almost didn't happen. In fact, it wasn't going to happen. I wasn't happy about it, but a year ago, there was nothing I could do but accept that Dean Seaborne's maiden voyage would also be his last. Fortunately, you did something. That's right. You. My readers. (If you're reading this, I'm assuming you're one of them). You guys went out and bought *The Lost Prince*, and you bought enough copies to send Dean off on another adventure. The only way I can repay you is with a good story. I hope I've done that here.

While we're at it, there are a few other people I need to thank:

My agent, Danielle Chiotti, who was there for me at a very tough time in my career, and whose guidance, support, and friendship are invaluable. I'm very lucky to have her, and everyone at Upstart Crow, in my corner.